ELOISE

ELOISE

CASE #3

Allie's Ghost Hunters

WITHDRAWN

CATHERINE JINKS

ALLEN & UNWIN

To Susan Allaburton
with gratitude

First published in 2003
This edition published in 2007

Allen & Unwin
83 Alexander St
Crows Nest NSW 2065
Australia
Phone: (61 2) 8425 0100
Fax: (61 2) 9906 2218
Email: info@allenandunwin.com
Web: www.allenandunwin.com

National Library of Australia
Cataloguing-in-Publication entry:

Jinks, Catherine, 1963–.
Eloise: a ghost story.

For ages 10–14.
ISBN 9781741146592.

1. Ghosts – Juvenile fiction. 2. Seances – Juvenile fiction. I. Title.
(Series: Jinks, Catherine, 1963– Allie's ghost hunters).

A823.3

Cover design by Tabitha King
Text design by Jo Hunt and Tabitha King
Set in 13 on 15.5pt Weiss by Midland Typesetters
Printed in Australia by McPherson's Printing Group

10 9 8 7 6 5 4 3 2 1

CHAPTER # one

It was all Michelle's fault. *I* never wanted to summon up spirits of the dead. I wouldn't have tried, if it hadn't been for the Exorcists' Club. And the Exorcists' Club was Michelle's idea.

'The Exorcists' Club?' I said doubtfully, when she first made the suggestion. 'What would that be for?'

'What do you think?' she replied. 'We'd go around getting rid of ghosts. *Exorcising* ghosts. For money.'

I stared at her. We were in the school library – as we generally are, at lunchtime. (We have to be, because we're library monitors, now.) And of course we weren't really supposed to be chatting away, though Mrs Procter doesn't mind a bit of noise as long as we keep our voices down and do our jobs. My job is putting books away. Michelle's job is looking after the computers. When no one's having trouble with the internet, or doing stupid things with a mouse pad, Michelle usually helps me.

She's my best friend, but that doesn't mean we always agree on everything.

'What makes you think we can get rid of ghosts?' I asked, and she clicked her tongue.

'You got rid of Eglantine, didn't you?' she said, as she shoved a copy of *The Silver Chair* firmly between *The Last Battle* and *The Voyage of the Dawn Treader*. 'Your house was haunted, and you got rid of the ghost. Not to mention that business at Hill End –'

'Yes, but hang on a minute.' I needed time to think. 'You told me once that you saw a film with an exorcist in it, and the exorcist was a priest.'

'I didn't see it. My cousin saw it.'

'Whatever.' I waved a book at her. 'My point is, the exorcist in that film was fighting a demon, wasn't he? It threw people out windows, and twisted their heads around, and made them speak in strange, spooky voices. That's what you said, isn't it?'

'Yes, but –'

'Eglantine didn't do any of those things. And we didn't *exorcise* her. You have to use prayers and things to exorcise something. Rituals.'

'No, you don't.'

'Yes, you do. I read it in a dictionary.'

So we went to look at *The Shorter Oxford English Dictionary*, which no one ever uses at our school – it's

2

disgraceful. Sure enough, the first definition of 'exorcise' was 'to drive out (an evil spirit) by the use of a holy name'.

'See?' I said. 'A holy name. I don't know how to do that. I wouldn't even want to.'

'Yes, but look at the second definition.' Michelle's forefinger stabbed at another line of print. '"To clear of evil spirits; to purify". There's nothing about holy names or rituals.'

'Eglantine wasn't an evil spirit. She was confused. As soon as we finished the story she was trying to write, she disappeared.'

'*Allie.*' Michelle was getting impatient. 'That isn't the point.'

'Shh!' I warned, with a quick glance at Mrs Procter's office. Obediently, Michelle lowered her voice.

'The point is, you're an expert, now,' she hissed. 'You know more about ghosts than practically anybody. So why not start a club?'

'Because I don't want to.' I'm not a clubby sort of person, you see. I'm not a joiner. But then Michelle cocked her head, and fixed me with a penetrating look.

'Peter wants to,' she said.

'Peter Cresciani?'

'Yup.'

'Oh.'

That made me pause. Don't get the wrong idea – it's not as if I have a crush on Peter, or anything. It's just that he's a friend of mine, and very intelligent, and if

3

he thinks that something is a good idea, then it's worth considering.

'You've talked to him about this?' I inquired, and Michelle nodded. 'What did he say?'

'He said he'd be interested in joining.'

'Really?'

'But only if you're in it.'

'When did he say that?'

'This morning. At recess.'

I had been chasing up lost property at recess: my brother's lost property, to be exact. Bethan never remembers to ask at the office when he's mislaid a hat or a drink bottle, so Mum makes me do it.

That lost-property box practically has his name on it.

'Well . . . I don't know,' I said. 'People already think I'm weird.'

'No, they don't.'

'Yes, they do.' People always think you're weird when you read lots of books, and keep a collection of animal skulls in your bedroom. A reputation for seeing ghosts only makes things worse. 'Is this going to be a *secret* club? I could handle a secret club.'

'Don't be silly. What would be the point of a secret club? We want people to contact us if they have any ghost problems.'

'People like who?'

'I don't know. Anybody.'

'People at school?'

'Perhaps. Or other people.'

I hesitated.

'It would just be us three,' Michelle went on. 'You, me and Peter. Most of it would be historical research. The way you did with Eglantine. Death certificates and stuff.'

'But we don't have any equipment,' I protested. When my family was trying to get rid of Eglantine, we used an organisation called PRISM (which stands for Paranormal Research Investigation Services and Monitoring). The PRISM people had brought to our house lots of different equipment: Geiger counters, electromagnetic field detectors, infra-red cameras. 'You need special equipment to detect the presence of a ghost.'

'Yes, but not for getting rid of a ghost. You got rid of Eglantine by working out what she wanted, and you did that by working out who she was.'

Michelle was right. I couldn't deny it. And I must admit that I had liked researching Eglantine's background. I'm one of those people who likes research projects. I can't help it. With a research project you get to play detective, only you're hunting down clues in libraries and on databases, instead of following footprints or getaway cars.

'We-e-ell . . .' I said.

'Come on, Allie. Please?' Michelle put on her fawning puppy act, panting and pressing her hands together at the wrist, like paws. It always annoys me – as she knows quite well, 'Pretty please?'

'Oh, stop.'

'*Please*, Allie?'

'All right, all right! I'll do it!'

Michelle beamed. It seemed a bit strange that she was so eager, but then again, she does have a tendency to get all enthusiastic about things. She's had big crushes on certain movies, and on decoupage, and on her piano teacher, and on the ballroom dancing classes that she was attending for a while with her mother. Not that most people realised how keen she was, at the time. She can be very cool and elegant, and doesn't jabber on about her latest fad, like some I could name. (Bethan, for instance.) On the contrary, she'll become rather silent, and intense, and focused. But I always pick up the signals.

It's occurred to me more than once that her crazes usually happen around the same time that her mum gets a new boyfriend. I won't go into that, however. It's not really my business.

'Okay,' she said. 'It's settled. So when do you want to have the first meeting? They should be regular – like every week.'

'Maybe we should talk to Peter, first. See what he thinks.'

'I s'pose.'

'If we're going to do it properly,' I continued, thinking hard, 'we should draw up a proper set of rules. About what our purpose is.'

'Our purpose is to get rid of ghosts.'

'Right. I know. But there has to be a procedure that we follow.'

Michelle nodded 'You mean, like, at what point do

we ask some of your PRISM friends to help us?' she suggested.

'I guess so. That sort of thing.'

'And whether we charge people money?'

'Yeah.' I nodded. 'That too.'

'And whether you call spirits up, instead of just getting rid of them?'

Michelle and I both jumped, because neither of us had asked this last question. It had come from Bettina Berich. She was standing right behind us, and we hadn't noticed her.

Michelle put a hand to her heart.

'God, Bettina!' she gasped. 'You scared the life out of me!'

'Sorry.'

'What are you doing, anyway?' Michelle's tone became a bit lofty and condescending. She can be like that, sometimes. 'This is a private conversation.'

'It's all right,' I said quickly, because I felt sorry for Bettina. It was awful the way some of the boys would tease her about her weight. 'You said yourself, Michelle, this isn't going to be a secret club.'

'Well, no, but –'

'What's up, Bettina? Sorry, I should be putting the rest of those books away.' There was still a big pile of them on the floor near the non-fiction shelves. 'My fault. Sorry.'

Bettina was another library monitor. It was odd that she should have been, because she wasn't all that fond of reading. I used to wonder if she had volunteered because she didn't like the playground at lunchtime. It can be a pretty nerve-racking place, if you're the target of a roaming pack of nasty loudmouths. And Bettina was certainly a target. Some of the really brainless kids would snatch food out of her hands, claiming that she ought to stop eating so much. They were exactly the same kids who flicked bits of sandwich or popcorn at her when she walked past.

And poor Bettina was shy, as well as large. What I mean is, she was hard to talk to. I had tried several times, but I never seemed to get very far. She would always nod frantically, and keep agreeing – unless you asked her a question. Then all you would get out of her was a 'yes' or a 'no'. She was quite new to the school, though, so perhaps she was finding her feet. That's what I told myself, when I saw her sitting alone at recess, picking at her Turkish bread. It helped to ease my pangs of guilt.

I wish I was a more sociable person. If I found it easier to say friendly, jolly things to people, I wouldn't have to go round feeling guilty about kids like Bettina.

'The bell's going to go any minute,' I remarked, checking the clock on the wall. 'We probably ought to straighten things up. Hey, who's been messing around with the medieval display? Michelle, look at this.'

'Wait!' said Bettina, and I stopped in my tracks. She looked anxious; she was squeezing her hands together. 'Wait,' she murmured. 'What about my question?'

'Eh?'

8

Bettina glanced nervously at Michelle, who was frowning. 'Well . . . you know about ghosts, don't you?' she quavered, but she was addressing me, not Michelle. 'Like . . . that's what you were talking about? Ghosts?'

I grunted. Michelle said, 'Yes.' Bettina fixed her big, brown eyes on us.

'Well, instead of getting rid of ghosts – like you were saying – what about making them appear?' she stammered. 'Would – would you be able to do that?'

I was lost. 'What do you mean?'

'I mean, if you wanted to talk to a ghost.' Bettina swallowed, and leaned towards me. 'Someone who'd died,' she added.

And then the bell went.

It's like a fire alarm or something, when the bell goes at school. Suddenly the corridors are filled with scurrying footsteps – people who are sitting, leap from their seats and there's a surge of chattering voices.

Over the noise, I said to Bettina: 'You want to talk to someone who's dead?'

'Yes.'

'Summon them up, you mean? From the afterlife?'

Bettina's uneasy gaze skipped around the room, as if reluctant to meet mine.

'I guess so,' she muttered, rubbing her arm.

'Who?' asked Michelle, and Bettina replied: 'My cousin.'

Michelle and I exchanged looks. Then a stampede of Year Four boys pushed past, and I staggered.

'We'll talk about it later,' I said loudly. 'You catch the bus, don't you? My bus?'

Bettina nodded.

'We'll talk on the bus, then.'

Bettina's face brightened. It occurred to me that she probably didn't have anyone to talk to on the bus, most days, and I felt bad. Then I told myself that she wasn't in my class, after all. It wasn't my fault that she didn't seem to have any friends.

Why didn't some of the other kids, like Peter Cresciani, make an effort?

CHAPTER # two

'Because she's dumb,' said Peter.

'Peter!' I protested, looking around quickly. But I couldn't see Bettina. She hadn't arrived at the bus line yet. 'Don't say that!'

Peter shrugged. 'It's true,' he insisted. 'I don't talk to Bettina because she's dumb. You should see her in class. She can never answer questions. She's in her own little world, most of the time.'

'Just because she daydreams doesn't mean she's dumb,' I said severely. That's the trouble with Peter. Most of the time he's really nice. He's also curious, clever, well read, and a little bit eccentric (which I like). But because he's so clever, he doesn't have much patience with people who aren't as clever as he is.

'Anyway, she wants to talk to her dead cousin,'

I went on, not bothering to keep my voice down, because all around us kids lining up for the bus were shouting and fighting, and flicking things at each other. 'Michelle reckons that if we help Bettina, it would be a good job for this Exorcists' Club she's been talking about, but I don't think so. It's a whole different thing, isn't it? Summoning up ghosts. *I've* never done it.'

'A séance, you mean,' said Peter.

'What?'

'You've never done a séance? That's how you talk to ghosts. You hold a séance. I read about it, somewhere.' He knitted his brows. 'I can't remember where.'

Then Michelle appeared, with Bettina in tow. Poor Bettina kept flinching at every scream and scuffle. Michelle just scowled at the kids who jostled her, and jabbed them in the ribs with her elbow.

'So,' she asked me, 'have you told Peter?'

'Yes, but –'

'It's worth trying, don't you think? Bettina was just explaining what the problem is. It's her cousin, you see – his name was Michael – and he was only seventeen when he died in a car accident. That was nearly two years ago. But her aunt is still crying about it.'

Michelle sounded a bit too eager and enthusiastic. Bettina, I saw, was standing with her eyes cast down. She let Michelle do all the talking.

'So Bettina wants to see if we can contact Michael (wherever he is) and maybe even get him to say a few words to her aunt,' Michelle continued. 'To make her aunt feel better.'

Suddenly Tony Karavias went careering into Bettina, knocking her sideways. (God knows what he was doing.) He didn't say sorry, of course – they never do, boys like that – he just laughed and threw himself at somebody else. Peter shouted after him, angrily: 'Watch what you're doing, ya moron!' He hates that kind of thing. Even when it happens to 'dumb' people.

Bettina picked up the bag that she'd dropped, and tucked a wisp of hair behind her ear.

'Okay,' said Michelle, turning back to me. 'What do you think? Can we do it?'

'I dunno.' The whole thing worried me. 'The question is, do we *want* to do it? I mean, I sympathise, and everything – I'm really sorry about your cousin, Bettina – but calling up ghosts . . .' I shook my head. 'That could be pretty dangerous, don't you think?'

Although I was appealing to Peter, it was Bettina who replied.

'Oh, no!' she assured me. 'Michael was a good person. He wouldn't do anything bad.'

'Well, maybe not, but –'

'I just want to know if he's all right. If – if he's happy, and peaceful.' Her eyes filled with tears. 'Then maybe Auntie Astra . . . maybe things will be better . . .' Her voice broke.

I didn't know where to look, when that happened. Peter stared at his shoes. Michelle screwed up her nose, and cleared her throat. There was nothing much else to say, really. How could I tell Bettina that we wouldn't give it a try? The poor girl looked so unhappy. It would have been mean to turn her down.

'Okay,' I sighed. 'We'll see what we can do.'

'Thanks,' Bettina sniffed.

'Though you shouldn't get your hopes up. We probably won't be able to help.' I scratched my head. 'Talking to dead people? I wouldn't know where to start.'

'With a séance,' said Peter, promptly. 'I told you.'

'Yeah, but what *is* a séance? Exactly?'

'It's . . . well, it's where you sit around. In a circle,' Peter replied.

'And do what?'

A pause. Someone's shoe went sailing over our heads, followed by screams of outrage.

'I don't know,' Peter admitted at last. 'Hold hands, I think.'

'We'll look it up,' I declared. 'Do some research. Don't worry, Bettina.' I nodded at her, and she blinked back at me. 'We'll do our best.'

Then the line began to move, and we all climbed onto the bus. Peter and Michelle and I aren't natural pushers and shovers, so we didn't manage to bag any seats together. I ended up sitting beside Tammy Ng, with Michelle just behind me. Peter was stuck next to some Year Four kid, and Bettina, poor thing, had to sit next to my brother. (My brother is not someone you want to sit next to on a bus trip, because he simply won't keep

14

still, wriggling about as if his pants are on fire. Mum used to think he had worms all the time, but we've come to realise that it's not worms. It's just Bethan.) Anyway, thanks to the seating arrangements, nothing more was said about the Exorcists' Club on that trip.

Michelle and I, however, get off at the same bus stop. That's why we were able to come to an agreement about Bettina's problem before we finally parted. I told her that I would see what I could find out about séances, and that I would even ask Delora Starburn for advice. Delora is the psychic who helped us to get rid of Eglantine. 'Delora,' I said, 'would probably know something about séances.'

'But if she tells me that we shouldn't be messing with spirits of the dead,' I added, 'then we'll stop. I mean it, Michelle. What happens if we call up this ghost, and it won't go away? You've never lived in a haunted house. You don't know what it's like.'

'Okay,' Michelle agreed. 'If it's dangerous, we'll stop.'

'The same thing with exorcisms. You told me the priest in that movie got killed, trying to exorcise a demon. I don't want that happening to any of *us*.'

'No, no,' said Michelle 'It's all right. We won't do anything stupid.'

She sounded suspiciously meek. But by that time we had reached her turn-off, so I couldn't press her for a 'cross-my-heart' promise. I could only shoot her a stern look, and wave her goodbye.

Seven minutes later, I was walking through my front door, with Bethan trailing about ten metres behind. He likes to pretend that we're not related when we're walking home from the bus stop (because a lot of his friends live nearby). Some sisters might be offended by this, but not me. In a funny kind of way, he's even doing me a favour, especially when he's been chucking water bombs about, or trying to kickbox lampposts. When that happens, he's as big an embarrassment to me as I am to him.

Put it this way: we have an understanding.

'Hi, Mum!' I shouted, as I banged into the kitchen – and stopped short.

There, sitting at the kitchen table, was my dad.

My *real* dad.

Let me explain, because I know this is a bit complicated. I've had a couple of 'dads' since my real dad left, though I never called any of them 'Dad' (if you know what I mean). First there was Simon, who moved in for about two years. I don't remember him very well. Now there's Ray, who's lived with us since I was six. I like Ray. Mum met him when she was modelling for a life-drawing class. He buys me books for my birthday, and always knocks before entering my room.

When I walked into the kitchen, Ray was on his feet, leaning against the fridge with his arms folded. My mum was perched up on the high stool, looking worried.

Dad didn't look worried. He looked tired and messy, but not worried. I recognised him instantly from the photo beside my bed, even though I hadn't seen him since . . . well, since I was four. He's been living in Thailand, you see. Usually, when he sends a photograph, it shows him wearing shorts and a singlet, maybe a hat – once a sarong – and with a bristly beard. It was strange to see him dressed in long, baggy pants (khaki-coloured) and a knitted jumper. It was even stranger to see him at all, in the flesh.

But I *had* been warned. Several times, during his monthly phone calls, Dad had mentioned that he wanted to come home. He had even written to Mum about it. She had told us (in the special voice she uses when she talks about my dad) that he wanted to visit us, and was interested in having us visit him, too, but that it would be entirely up to my brother and me. It would be our decision. 'I'm quite happy for you to get acquainted with him,' Mum had announced. 'He is your father, after all, though he hasn't exactly put much effort into it lately. He does say, however, that he regrets not working on his relationship with his children, so perhaps he's trying to do the right thing. Disperse the negative *chi*, so to speak. Anyway, as I said, it's up to you.'

So it wasn't as if I hadn't been notified. The trouble was, I hadn't believed that my father would actually show up. Not really. When I was little, I must have been told a thousand times that I would be seeing him

17

soon; that he would be sending money, so I could fly to Thailand; that he would be coming home for Christmas; that we would all go on holiday together, Bethan and Dad and I. He always used to say things like that, and it never happened. He would phone me, and send me presents, and sometimes even write me letters, but he would never appear.

And now suddenly, out of the blue, he had.

'Alethea,' he said, rising from his chair. 'Hello, sweetheart.'

Alethea. That's my name – Alethea Gebhardt. It was Dad's idea, though Mum was happy about it because she's a bit of a hippy, at heart. However, she now calls me 'Allie', like everyone else around here, and it's only Dad who insists on using my full name.

Not that I mind my full name, exactly, but . . . oh, I don't know. It sounds like something out of *The Lord of the Rings*, or a Star Wars movie. And everyone thinks I'm weird enough as it is.

'Hello, Dad,' I said cautiously, stiffening up as he hugged me tight. He smelled funny, like one of Mum's incense sticks.

'Where's Bethan?' he asked, releasing his grip, and I gestured over my shoulder.

'Coming,' I replied. 'He's coming.' Then I wriggled out of Dad's embrace and chucked my bag on the floor. 'Um – can I have a drink?'

'Yes, of course,' said Mum, slipping down from her stool. But it was Ray who opened the top cupboard for me, and pulled out a glass. Mum added sarcastically: 'Your father's just *dropped in*, as you can see. Perhaps he didn't realise that Ray would be home sick, today.'

Ray coughed into a handkerchief as he poured me an orange juice; he had a terrible cold. Normally, he's very neat and well groomed. In fact, you wouldn't think that he was an artist, because he wears glasses, and cuts his hair short, and irons his jeans as well as his shirts, and takes a briefcase to his drawing job at the Department of Forestry. That day, however, he looked creased and tousled – rather like my dad, actually, except that he's not as tall or as hairy as my dad.

'I'm glad we could meet, at last,' Ray said mildly, wiping his nose. 'Ah. That sounds like Bethan, now. We'd better break out the Anzac biscuits.'

Poor Bethan. He really blew it, because he didn't recognise Dad at all. He pounded in, made straight for the biscuit barrel, and began pleading for something to drink. He barely glanced at Dad. When Dad said 'Bethan', he had to say it twice before my brother turned around, wide-eyed, his mouth full of biscuit.

'It's your dad, Bethan,' Mum sighed. 'Your dad's dropped in.'

Chewing, Bethan stared at Dad. Then he said: 'Oh.'

'How are ya, mate?' Dad asked gently. 'How's school?'

'Okay,' Bethan replied, spraying crumbs. He shot me an apprehensive look. I could tell that he was dying to get away.

'How would you feel about coming out to dinner with me?' Dad inquired, adding: 'Both of you? We could go anywhere you wanted.'

'You mean McDonald's?' said Bethan, brightening. We never go to McDonald's; Mum doesn't believe in it.

'Oh . . . ah . . . well, I don't think so,' Dad stammered, and Mum cut in.

'Not McDonald's, Bethan. You know that.'

Bethan's face fell. I said: 'So we can't really go anywhere we want?'

'Anywhere but McDonald's,' Dad amended.

'Burger King?'

'Well . . . yes, I suppose so, but –'

'Pizza Hut?'

'If you really want to, Alethea, but there are other kinds of food in the world besides American junk,' Dad pointed out. 'There's a great place in Newtown, near where I'm staying, and it has a kind of smorgasbord of Indian food. Chicken tandoori and naan bread, lentils, curry puffs . . . you can choose whatever you want. I'm sure you'd like it.'

Again, Bethan and I exchanged glances. Then we shook our heads. Mum had tried to make us eat curry in the past. It had burned our tongues.

'No,' we chorused.

'Thai, then. I know all about Thai food. I know just what you'd like.'

'We like kebabs,' I said cautiously.

20

'Lebanese? All right. We'll try something along those lines.'

In the end, we went to an Egyptian restaurant, where they served a kind of lamb stew, which was all right, and okra, which wasn't. We went that night, even though it was a school night; Mum said that she didn't mind, if we didn't mind. I thought it was the right thing to do. Bethan liked the idea because he expected an Egyptian restaurant to have life-sized mummies (or photographs of mummies) as part of the decoration.

He was very disappointed when we arrived, because there wasn't a mummy to be seen. Just hieroglyphs painted on the walls, and a cat sculpture near the window.

There weren't any other people eating there, either. Dad suggested that it was perhaps a little early.

'So,' he added, 'I guess you must be wondering why I've shown up like this, out of the blue? Must be a bit of a shock?'

'Sort of,' I mumbled. Bethan just stared blankly. The thing about Bethan is, he doesn't really give much thought to the adults in his life, or why they do what they do. He's interested in football and skateboarding and karate and magic tricks and horror stories and kickboxing. Everything else, he pretty much ignores.

Most eight-year-old boys are like this, in my experience. At least, Bethan's friends certainly are.

'The thing is, I've been on a long search for meaning,' my dad said. 'That's why I went to Thailand in the first place. I wasn't easy in my mind about a lot of things. I had a lot of questions that hadn't been answered here in Australia, and I think I was lost. Confused. You know, my upbringing was very strict, I had a lot of issues that I hadn't resolved, and I felt stifled, and angry – angry at myself, really, though I took it out on other people, like your mum, for example . . . It wasn't right. I know that now. I had to come to terms with myself, get in touch with myself, and that's what I've been doing, all these years . . .'

Dad explained that he had learned all sorts of things in Thailand, like how to meditate (properly), how to relate to other people, how to be honest with himself as well as others. Most importantly, he had learned how to recognise his own faults.

'I realised that when I left you kids here in Australia, I had cut off something vital within myself. It was like cutting off a leg or an arm. At the time, I didn't understand, but I was damaging all of us. And I'm sorry.' Dad reached across the table. 'I'm sorry, kids. I've come back to say I'm sorry.'

It was very confusing. On the one hand, I felt like crying. On the other hand, I knew exactly why Bethan was squirming in his seat beside me. Bethan hates it when things get 'heavy'. You should see him whenever Mum tries to explain how precious we are to her – he goes as red as his hair.

'It's all right,' I mumbled.

'No, it's not,' Dad declared. 'It's not all right. I cast

you out of my life, effectively, and that was wrong. I have to correct that mistake. You *are* part of my life and you're going to *be* part of my life. I won't shut you out any more.'

Then the food arrived. As well as the lamb stew and the okra, there was something made out of chickpeas and something made out of spinach. Dad didn't eat the lamb: he said he was a vegetarian. He also said that he would be importing Thai fabrics and leathergoods into Australia while he put together an 'exhibition'. Dad's a photographer, you see: he takes ordinary photos, which he calls 'business', and photos that he turns into screen-prints and collages and ceramic plaques, which he calls 'art'.

'I have a friend named Matoaka, and she's a fabric artist,' he told us. 'She works with silk, and she's been helping me transfer my images onto silk. It's very effective. She's very talented.'

'Is she from Thailand?' I asked.

'Well – no, originally she's from Brisbane. Though she has lived in Thailand for several years.' Dad cleared his throat. 'As a matter of fact, she's come back to Australia, too. We're living with a friend of hers, in Newtown.'

'Oh.' So Dad had a girlfriend. I wasn't really surprised, though he hadn't mentioned her before.

'She wants to meet you kids very much,' Dad continued. 'She wants to cook you dinner, some time on the weekend. How about Friday night? Or Saturday? Probably Friday.'

23

Bethan shrugged. I grunted. I also made a mental note: no meeting of the Exorcists' Club on Friday night.

'Do you kids know Newtown at all? It's an interesting place. Very vibrant. Very questing. A bit exhausting, sometimes – the energy isn't completely aligned, I would say – but if you have to live in the city, there are worse places. Personally, I'd prefer something up north, on the beach, but we haven't got that far with our arrangements.' Dad saw that Bethan wanted to say something, and smiled at him. 'What's up, mate?'

'Can I have ice-cream?' Bethan wanted to know, I kicked him. 'Please?' he added.

'Oh, I'm not sure.' Dad peered around, but the menus were stacked on the other side of the room. 'They probably have baklava,' he said.

'Ice-cream would be better.'

'Do you think so? Have you ever tried baklava? I think you'd like it.'

He was wrong, actually. Bethan tried the baklava, and didn't like it. (I did.) But, as I said to Bethan later, we had to give Dad a chance.

After all, he didn't really know us. Any more than we knew him.

CHAPTER # three

The next morning, as we walked to the bus stop, Bethan didn't lag behind me. He wasn't trying to pretend that I didn't exist. Instead of dawdling ten paces to my rear, dragging a stick along a fence or snapping agapanthus flowers off their stalks, he hurried to catch up, his overloaded bag bouncing around on his back.

'Hey,' he panted.

'What?'

'Hang on.'

'Your shoelace is undone.'

He's still not very good at tying shoelaces, so they're always coming undone. I didn't bother to wait, of course; normally he doesn't want me to. But this time was different.

'Stop!' he yelped.

'Why?'

'Because!'

I stopped. I waited. At last he joined me, looking red in the face. I regarded him curiously.

'What is it?' I asked. He hadn't been in trouble that morning. We hadn't been fighting. He wasn't interested in any of my possessions. Why did he particularly want to talk to me – and on our way to school? Our bus stop was only down the street; one of his friends might see him in conversation with a *big sister*. 'Are you feeling sick?'

'You know how Dad's come back?'

Ah. So that was it. I'd been thinking about Dad myself, as a matter of fact. Quite a lot.

'What about it?' I said cautiously.

'Well . . . does that mean we'll have to go and live with him?'

You won't believe it, but that possibility had never even occurred to me. For a moment I stood staring at him, with my mouth hanging open. Then I swallowed.

'No,' I replied.

'Are you sure?'

'I'm sure.'

I wasn't, to tell you the truth, but I didn't want Bethan to worry. When Bethan worries, he tends to play up. Besides, I knew that Mum would never let us move away for good. The most she'd put up with would be the odd visit. Maybe once a month?

As Bethan skipped ahead of me, his concerns laid

to rest, I wondered if I should ask someone about shared living arrangements. Not Michelle; she didn't have to worry about her father. He had disappeared before she was born. And Peter's parents were still married. He wouldn't know anything.

I didn't really want to ask Mum. If I did, she would fret, and want to talk and talk about it all.

But I probably wouldn't have any choice.

'So, did you ring Delora?' was the first thing Michelle said when I arrived at the bus stop. It took me a moment to remember who Delora was. My head was full of other things.

'Uh – no.' I had forgotten all about my promise. 'Something came up. Sorry.' I was about to explain, but decided not to. There were people around, the bus was about to arrive, and anyway, it was a funny situation. I had to think about it before I discussed it. I wanted to work out how I felt.

Michelle, I knew, thought my dad was like her dad. She didn't have any patience with either of them. She would probably say that I should tell my dad to piss off.

I wasn't sure if I wanted to hear her say that. In fact, I didn't feel like talking about Dad at all. The whole subject was too difficult. So I shoved it to the back of my mind.

'I'll call tonight,' I assured Michelle. 'And today I'll do some research. In the library, at lunchtime. I'll find out what I can about séances.'

Which was quite a lot, in the end. While Michelle struggled with a very slow internet server, trying to connect with various paranormal web pages, I looked up 'séance' in everything that I could find. The most useful source was a two-volume set called *The Encyclopaedia of the Paranormal*.

I got five pages of notes out of that book.

'Okay,' I declared, upon rejoining Michelle (who was still waiting on a download). 'First of all, Peter was right. The definition of a séance is "a sitting organised for the purpose of receiving spirit communications or paranormal manifestations via the services of a medium".'

'Via what?' said Michelle.

'Via the services of a medium.' I checked my notes. 'A medium is someone who can see and talk with the dead, and even allow his or her body to be taken over by disembodied spirits.'

'Eugh.' Michelle made a face. 'I don't like the sound of *that*.'

I shrugged as Bettina drifted over to us. She had been shelving books for me. 'It mightn't be so bad,' I said. 'Delora Starburn let Eglantine take over her body when she wrote down the end of Eglantine's book. I didn't actually see it happen, but it can't have been as bad as it sounds.'

'So Delora is a medium?' Michelle asked.

'I guess so.' On reflection, she probably was. 'None of *us* are, that's for sure.'

'And we can't hold a séance without a medium?'

'I don't know. Probably not.'

'Bum,' said Michelle.

Bettina, frowning, inquired what the matter was.

'Oh, we need someone special if we want to hold a séance,' I explained. 'Someone like my friend Delora. A psychic.'

'Can you talk to her?' Bettina entreated. 'See if she can help us?'

'Yeah. I guess so.'

'What else did you find out?' Michelle demanded.

I gave her a quick rundown. With any 'sitting', I had discovered, there should be no more than eight 'sitters'. Younger sitters seemed to exude a 'more favourable psychic attraction' than older ones . . .

'Oh, good,' said Michelle.

'. . . but places steeped in colourful history make better locations for any séance,' I finished in a glum voice. 'I don't know anywhere around here with a "colourful history", do you? Except the Hyde Park Barracks. Convicts used to sleep in there.' We had visited the barracks on a school excursion. 'Trouble is, I don't think they'd let us hold a séance in a museum.'

'No, no,' Bettina interrupted. 'We want to talk to Michael, not a convict. Michael never went to the Hyde Park Barracks.'

She had a point. Michelle began to gnaw at her thumbnail. I cleared my throat, and said: 'Where did your cousin die, Bettina? In a hospital?'

It was awful to see Bettina's eyes fill with tears again. I hated myself for asking such a stupid question, and was about to withdraw it when Bettina replied: 'On the Pacific Highway. Near Gosford.'

'Oh.' So *that* was no good. I couldn't see us sitting around by the side of a road, trying to summon up a spirit as semi-trailers roared by. I even felt a bit queasy at the thought of visiting the actual spot.

Suddenly, for the first time, it occurred to me that someone had really *died*. All mangled up, probably, and trapped in a car wreck.

'Maybe we shouldn't do this . . .' I began.

'Wait.' Michelle grabbed my arm. 'What about his house? Michael's house? Where he used to live? That might work.'

I hesitated. Yes, I thought, but do we really want it to work?

'We can't go to Michael's house,' said Bettina, wiping her eyes. 'He used to live with my auntie in a flat, but she lives with us now. And he died before we moved.'

'Oh.' Another brick wall. 'Never mind. I'll see what Delora says. She might have a suggestion.' At that moment, the bell rang. 'I'll call her tonight,' I promised, heading for the door. 'She's bound to know what we should do.'

Delora, in fact, was most sympathetic. When I called her, she accepted my desire to hold a séance as if it were the most natural thing in the world. She and her sisters, she informed me, had held them all the time.

'When we were kids,' she squawked. 'At the dining-room table.'

'Did they work?'

'Oh, sometimes.' A couple of hacking coughs. (Delora smokes.) 'Yeah, we got through once or twice.'

'Talked to dead people, you mean?'

'Oh, well, sweetie, you know me,' said Delora. 'I can't get away from dead people. No, we were more inter-ested in the physical side. Raising tables, that kind of stuff.'

'And did you? Raise a table, I mean.'

'We cracked a wall,' Delora chuckled. 'I remember that. Bloody great crack went running down the wall. Mum was furious.'

'But what about the spirits?' I pressed. 'If my friends and I sat around a table, holding hands, would we be able to talk to Bettina's cousin?'

Another barrage of coughs. 'Aah,' Delora moaned. 'Oh. 'Scuse me, love, bit of a chest at the moment. What was that?'

'I *said*, if my friends and I hold a séance, would we be able to talk to Bettina's dead cousin? By ourselves?'

'Well, maybe.' Delora didn't sound too encouraging. 'It's possible.'

'So we wouldn't need a medium?'

Delora sighed – and coughed. 'Darl, you've got to understand, sittings aren't always successful. You have to have the right combination of elements.'

'Like what?'

'Well, a receptive group, a decent venue – not too much ornament – a lot of patience. And the right kind of channeller. Someone with an open mind.'

'Like you?'

Delora chuckled. 'Like me. Sure,' she said.

'Could *you* do it for us? Contact Bettina's cousin? Could you be our medium?'

'Ah.' I heard a *click-click-click* and a long hiss. I wondered if Delora had just lit another cigarette. 'The thing is, sweetie – I mean, you have to understand – that's my livelihood.' For once, she seemed a little embarrassed. 'That's what I do for a living, contact spirits. I can't just . . . if it gets around that I've been doing it for free, well, how could I go on charging people? Do you see what I'm saying?'

'Oh.' Of course. Delora was a *professional* psychic. I had forgotten. 'So how much do you charge?'

'Sixty an hour.'

Sixty dollars! An *hour*! I nearly fell off my chair.

'For you, though, forty,' she continued. 'Friend's discount.'

'Oh – well – er, thanks.' I was still gasping for breath. 'I'm, um, I'll think about it. Maybe we'll try it ourselves, first.'

'That's right. You do that,' Delora said cheerfully. 'You might get a result, why not? I remember reading about some kids in America, back in the 1930s; *they* used to get all kinds of results without a medium: raps, spirit writing, psychic photos, levitations. I've always said you've got a dark aura, Allie. There's something about your energy patterns – channelling should be simple for you. Just sit down, empty your mind and focus.'

'Er, okay.'

'And don't forget the personal possession. Remember Eglantine's book? If you're trying to contact someone *specific*, always track down one of their personal possessions first. Otherwise,' another wheezy laugh, 'otherwise you could end up connecting with Teddy Roosevelt!'

I didn't ask who Teddy Roosevelt was. Instead, very quickly (because I could hear Mum calling me to dinner), I sought reassurance.

'It won't be dangerous?' I gabbled. 'There won't be any risks?'

'Risks? Of course! You take a risk every time you cross the road.' I could almost see her shrug. 'What *you* have to do is decide whether the risks are worth the result.'

Great. So it was *my* decision. I went to dinner and chewed over Delora's advice while I munched on Ray's vegetarian stir-fry. I didn't know what to do. Try the séance without Delora? Raise forty dollars, somehow? Call the whole thing off? I was unsure of what to expect if we did go ahead, and we were successful. Would Michael's ghost suddenly appear? Would one of us start to talk in Michael's voice? Or would we simply get tables flying around, and cracks appearing on the wall?

'This is good, Ray,' said Mum. 'Delicious.'

33

'I used fresh herbs, this time.'

'Lovely. You're such a great cook.'

Ray grunted. He was looking better, but not a lot better. There were dark circles under his eyes, and his expression was glum.

I wondered: would *I* be the one who ended up talking in Michael's voice? Delora had referred to my 'energy patterns'. Would Michael's ghost find them attractive? If a ghost ever entered *my* body, I would die. I would lie down and die of terror.

On the other hand, as Delora had said, sittings weren't always successful. The chances that we would actually call up Michael's spirit were pretty remote. Especially without Delora to help us.

I decided that, if something bad started to happen, I would signal Peter to jump up and turn on the light.

'Mum?' I said.

'Mmmm?'

Can I go to a friend's house, tomorrow afternoon? It's not far away. I'll be home for dinner.'

'What friend?' asked Mum. 'Michelle, you mean?'

'No. You don't know her. She catches my bus.'

'What's her name?' said Mum, adding: 'Don't mess around with your food, Bethan – just eat it.'

'I'm full,' Bethan complained, as if being full was some kind of painful disease, and Mum had infected him with it. 'I can't eat any more.'

'Well, you're not getting any dessert. Not unless you eat more.'

Bethan mumbled something. I said loudly: 'Her name is Bettina. Bettina Berich. She only came to our school this year.'

'Bettina Berich?' Mum seemed slightly distracted. I think she was still worrying about Bethan's stomach. 'Have I met her?'

'No,' I replied patiently. 'That's what I said. You haven't.'

'She's the big fat one,' said Bethan.

'*Bethan!*' We all rounded on him, Mum more quickly than the rest of us. 'Don't talk about people like that, please,' she frowned. 'You know what I've told you.'

'She's a nice person,' I said. 'You shouldn't judge people by what they look like.'

'Our modern standards of appearance are very unrealistic,' Ray pointed out, in a croaky voice. 'They're shaped by air-brushed photos and digitalised images. Especially in the case of young girls.'

Bethan stuck out his bottom lip. 'Fat people eat too much,' he growled. 'I don't want to eat any more. I don't want to get fat.'

'You won't get fat, Bethan,' Mum smiled. I smiled, too, because if Bethan was any thinner, he'd be able to slip under the door. 'You certainly won't get fat eating Ray's stir-fry. Tofu's one of the healthiest foods there is.'

'I hate tofu,' said Bethan. Clearly, he was in one of his moods. (He loathes being jumped on.) Mum, however, just raised her eyebrows.

35

'I'm sensing thunder energy at this table,' she said in a sing-song voice, withdrawing her attention from my brother and assuming the kind of serene expression she always puts on, when she starts to use Feng Shui terms. 'Can you feel it, Ray? I think someone needs their *chi* aligned, don't you?'

'Why can't we have more meat?' Bethan went on, stubbornly.

'I think someone might need to meditate in his room for a little while.'

'Dad lets us eat meat.'

Bethan's words seemed to hit the table with a thud. Mum's serene expression disappeared; she was left looking cross and impatient. Ray focused his eyes on the tablecloth. I squirmed in my seat, because I knew exactly what Bethan was doing, and I didn't want Mum getting all fired up. Not when I was seeking permission to go to Bettina's house.

'You know quite well,' Mum snapped at Bethan, 'that your father is a vegetarian.'

'Yeah, but he lets *us* eat meat.'

'So do I, Bethan!'

'Then why can't we have chicken with this, sometimes? Instead of tofu?'

'I can always add chicken,' Ray began quietly. 'It wouldn't be –'

'You're the cook, Ray!' Mum interrupted. 'If you want to make a vegetarian stir-fry, then you can make a vegetarian stir-fry! Since you're doing us a *favour*, we'll eat

36

whatever you want us to eat!' Mum began to stab at the food with her fork. 'When the day comes that you cook us all a lamb roast, Bethan, we'll gladly abide by your decision. Until then, you'll have to put up with what you get. Okay?'

Inwardly, I groaned. My brother had really touched a nerve, for some reason – even Bethan, I could see, was slightly surprised – and I still hadn't got an answer out of Mum.

'So can I go, Mum?' I asked.

'What?'

'To Bettina's place. Can I go?'

'Oh, I don't know.' She sounded fed up. 'I suppose so. How will you get there?'

'By bus. We catch the same bus,' I reminded her. 'It's in that street with the pre-school on the corner. You know? Number 27.'

'All right, but how will you get home?'

'I'll pick her up,' Ray interjected. 'Don't worry. I'll pick her up after work.'

'Are you sure?' Mum's forehead puckered. 'It seems like a lot of trouble.'

'It's no trouble.'

'Are you sure?'

'I'm sure.'

'You don't have to.'

'I want to. Really.' Ray looked at Mum over the top of his glasses. 'Unless you have some objection?'

'I didn't say that.'

Silence. Ray very carefully rolled noodles around his fork.

'Ray?' said Mum. 'What are you getting at?'

'What are *you* getting at?'

'Nothing.'

'Good.'

'There's no reason to worry,' Mum insisted. 'You mustn't worry.'

'I'm not.'

'You're as much a part of our lives as you ever were.'

Ray snorted. I tuned out. It was all a bit over my head, and I had other things to think about.

Delora, for instance. She had advised that the right sort of venue for a séance shouldn't have much 'ornament'. But what would she classify as 'ornament', I wondered. Frilly lampshades? Printed quilt covers? Fancy door handles?

There were still many things that I had to settle, one way or another.

CHAPTER # four

Bettina's house was made of bright red brick, with iron bars on the windows and red tiles on the roof. The garden was mostly paved over with cement. Inside, it was a bit grimy, but not because Bettina's mum didn't clean. According to Bettina, her mum hadn't been able to get all the mould out of the bathroom, or the brownish smoke stains off the ceiling, or even some of the marks off the carpet, but she had tried her best. The kitchen was tidier than ours. The living room was also extremely neat – perhaps because there wasn't much furniture in it. The room contained one vinyl couch, an armchair, and an entertainment unit. Behind the glass doors of the entertainment unit were a television and video player; on its top was a collection of photographs in silvery frames, a couple of trophies, a wooden cheeseboard, a baseball cap and a hand-drawn birthday card.

'That's Michael,' said Bettina, pointing at the photographs. 'Those are the two swimming trophies he won at school, and that's the cheeseboard he made in woodwork, and that's the birthday card he drew for Auntie Astra –'

'And that's his baseball cap,' Michelle finished, before Bettina could. 'Did he wear that?'

'Yes. All the time.'

'Can we use it for the séance?' I asked.

'Maybe.' Bettina glanced over her shoulder. 'We'd better not touch anything unless my auntie says we can.'

'But she's not here,' Michelle protested. 'You said she's not here.'

'She's not,' Bettina agreed. In fact, her mum and aunt were both at work; Bettina always let herself into the house, after school, with her very own front-door key. I hadn't known this, before arriving. If I had, Mum probably wouldn't have let me come.

Bettina's sister, Josie (who went to high school), was supposed to rush straight home every afternoon, and take care of Bettina. She almost never did, though. According to Bettina, Josie had a very busy social life.

'No one's going to know that we've touched anything,' I remarked. 'We'll put it back before your aunt comes home. When does she come home?'

'In about two hours,' Bettina replied. 'After my mum gets here.'

40

'Is that your mum?' asked Peter, gesturing at a large, framed photograph that was hanging on the wall. There were other photographs, too, but this was the largest; it showed two women and three children, against a blue backdrop. One woman was dressed in black. The other was dressed in red. They looked alike.

'No, that's my auntie,' said Bettina. 'That's Michael standing behind her.'

'Is that *you*?' Peter sounded faintly surprised.

'Yes. It was taken three years ago.'

In the photograph, Bettina looked quite thin. There were dimples on each side of her smile. Her sister, on the other hand, was pouting.

'Is this your dad?' Michelle suddenly inquired. She had found a little picture hanging on the wall by itself, near the door.

'That's Michael's dad,' Bettina responded shortly. 'He died.'

'In the same accident?'

'No. A long time ago.'

'What about *your* dad?'

There was a brief silence. Realising that Bettina probably didn't want to talk about her dad, I opened my mouth to interrupt. But Michelle beat me to it.

'My dad left my mum,' she revealed carelessly, peering hard at the portrait of Bettina's uncle. 'So did Allie's. Is that what happened with your parents, too?'

'Yeah,' Bettina admitted, and might have said more, if Peter hadn't jumped in. He doesn't seem to like

41

people talking about their parents splitting up. He probably feels left out, because his own mum and dad are still together.

'Okay,' he interjected. 'So where will we do this? In here? We could close the blinds.'

'In my bedroom,' Bettina decided. 'Just in case Josie comes home.'

'All right. Where's your bedroom?'

There were three bedrooms in Bettina's house, plus an enclosed verandah where Josie slept. It was spilling over with dog-eared textbooks and skimpy clothes and beat-up old wardrobes and empty cassette-tape boxes. Bettina slept in the smallest bedroom, which was only big enough to fit in one single bed and a chest of drawers. Looking around, I saw that the light-shade was made out of plain, white paper; that the carpet was orange; that there were venetian blinds at the window and a simple green quilt on the bed. The only clutter was under the bed, and on top of the chest of drawers.

But clutter, I decided – especially Bettina's clutter – wasn't the same as ornament. There were no discarded bracelets or china figurines scattered around her room. All I could see were hairclips, exercise books, dirty plates, balls of screwed-up clothes, empty chewing gum wrappers, cassette tapes and dead flowers.

'Good,' I said. 'No ornament.'

'But we can't fit a table in here,' Peter objected.

'We don't have to. We don't *have* to sit around a table.

We can sit in a circle on the floor. There's enough room – there's only four of us.'

So we shut the door, closed the blinds, and sat down. It wasn't really dark, just dim. But that didn't matter, I assured everyone. Some mediums were known to work in full light.

'Now what?' asked Peter.

'Now we hold hands,' I replied.

'Activate the mind meld,' Peter intoned. (He has a tendency to drop into sci-fi speak without warning.) 'Let's all merge on the atomic level.'

His hands were hot and sweaty. Michelle's were cool and dry. I don't know what Bettina's were like, because I wasn't sitting next to her.

Someone's stomach rumbled.

'Okay,' I said. 'Now we open with songs and prayers.'

'Songs and *prayers!*' Peter exclaimed.

'Like the Lord's Prayer. Does anyone know the Lord's Prayer? Apparently, people usually start with the Lord's Prayer.'

It turned out that everyone in the room knew the Lord's Prayer, except me. They recited it. Then Peter recited two other prayers.

'I should have brought my mum's missal,' he concluded. 'She's got a million prayers in that book. She takes it to church every Sunday.'

'What about songs?' asked Michelle. 'What kind of songs should we be singing?'

'I'm not sure,' I had to confess. 'I couldn't find out.'

'Something soft,' Peter suggested. 'Nothing loud.'

'A lullaby,' said Bettina.

'What songs did Michael like?' I looked at Bettina, who swallowed. 'Think,' I urged her.

'Well . . .' She knitted her brows. 'He liked Smashing Pumpkins, Garbage, Pearl Jam.'

'Oh!' Peter's face brightened. 'I like Pearl Jam. I like that song "Alive".'

Michelle and I exchanged glances. We'd never heard of it.

'Can you sing it?' I asked Peter, who grimaced.

'I don't have to sing it, do I?' he groaned. 'You'll all laugh.'

'We won't laugh,' I promised.

'Cross your heart?'

'Cross my heart.'

Michelle and Bettina crossed their hearts, too. Then Peter sang a really depressing song about some bloke whose father died and who wanted to know if he deserved to die as well, and Bettina sang 'Cherry lips', because her sister often played it. (I don't know *what* that song was about.) Bettina had a pretty good voice, I thought. After she and Peter had finished, I addressed Michael directly, closing my eyes and tilting back my head.

'Michael,' I intoned. 'Can you hear me, Michael, son of Astra?'

Someone snickered, and I opened one eye.

'Stop it!'

'Sorry,' said Michelle, composing her features. 'Sorry, you sounded funny.'

'You do it, then!'

'No, no. I wouldn't know what to say.'

'Maybe we shouldn't say anything,' Peter proposed. 'Maybe we should all shut our eyes and breathe slowly and sort of see what happens.'

So we did. And nothing happened except that I started to feel hungry. My head filled with pictures of milkshakes and potato chips and fried rice. My stomach started to growl.

'Sorry,' I muttered. 'That was me.'

'Shh!'

We sat for a little while longer, before I suddenly remembered that we had forgotten Michael's cap. Bettina was sent to fetch it (and take careful note of its position, so that it could be restored to the exact same spot without upsetting anyone). When the cap was passed to me, I studied it, and smelled it (it smelled of dust) and placed it on my head. Then I shut my eyes and clasped my neighbours' hands again.

'We're awaiting you, Michael. Come, Michael,' I said. 'Your cousin awaits you.'

But it was no good. Nothing happened, not even after we'd placed one of Michael's photographs in the centre of our circle. After half an hour, my legs were cramping, my bladder was bursting, and my stomach was groaning. I couldn't concentrate. I was about to ask if we could wrap it up when Peter said, 'This is no good. This isn't going to work.'

'Just try,' Bettina pleaded. 'A little bit more.'

'I can't.' Peter shook his head. 'I'm starving. I have to have something to eat.'

'Me, too,' said Michelle. 'Is there something we can eat, Bettina?'

'Oh yes. Yes, you want food? I'll get you food.'

Bettina jumped up eagerly, and led the others into the kitchen. I went to the bathroom first. When I rejoined the group, everyone was already tucking into Saltines and olives and cream cheese and sultanas. Then Bettina made us each a big, peanut-butter sandwich and poured us huge glasses of milk. By the time we'd got all that down, we were starting to feel satisfied.

So we returned to her room and tried again. Having reminded the others that not every séance is successful, I plopped Michael's cap on top of his photograph, and focused my attention fiercely on both items. 'Close your eyes, Bettina,' I instructed. 'Think about Michael. Think about what he looked like. Think about what he used to do. Think about what he used to wear.'

Obediently, Bettina shut her eyes.

'The rest of you, look at the picture,' I said. 'Concentrate on the picture. The curly hair. The brown eyes. The crooked teeth –'

Bang! A sharp noise startled us all. I heard the sound of footsteps in the hall, and looked at Peter in alarm. But Bettina was saying: 'That's Josie. She's home.'

'*Bettina!*' a voice called. '*Where are you?*'

'I'm in here!'

'*What?*'

'*I'M IN HERE!*'

The bedroom door burst open. A girl with dark hair piled on top of her head and a very short uniform looked in. 'What the hell are you doing?' she demanded.

'Nothing,' Bettina mumbled.

'Ah!' Josie's gaze had snagged on the baseball cap. In gloating, triumphant tones, she began to rattle off words that I didn't understand. Bettina responded sharply in the same language.

They both snatched at the cap – which Josie managed to capture.

'You're in big trouble!' she cried gleefully.

'Give it back!' cried Bettina.

'I'm going to tell Auntie!'

Bettina chased her sister out of the bedroom; I could hear thumps and shrieks as they spilt down the hall and into the garden. A screen door slammed. Voices were raised.

Peter sighed.

'Well,' he said. 'I guess that's it, then.'

'We could try by ourselves,' I suggested.

'No. I don't feel like it.' Stiffly, Peter began to rise. 'As a matter of fact, I'm hungry again.'

'Me, too,' said Michelle. 'Do you think Bettina would mind if we had some more bread?'

Sighing, I realised that there was no point trying to hold a séance with people who were only interested in their stomachs. I also realised that I, too, could have done with a few more mouthfuls of peanut-butter sandwich. So I followed Michelle and Peter into the kitchen, where we made ourselves sandwiches, finished off the sultanas, and found a couple of apples.

We were still stuffing our mouths when Bettina returned from the backyard, sweaty and panting and very upset.

'She won't give it to me,' Bettina wailed. 'She says she's going to tell Auntie Astra.'

'Have a biscuit,' Michelle advised, sympathetically.

'It's all right, Bettina,' I said. 'We'll tell your aunt what we've been trying to do, and I'm sure she won't get mad.'

'Josie laughed,' Bettina went on. 'She says we're being stupid.'

'*You are!*' her sister bellowed, from the next room. (The enclosed verandah was right next to the kitchen; you had to pass through it to reach the backyard.) '*You're all crazy!*'

'Don't pay any attention,' Peter murmured. 'She's only trying to annoy you. My brothers do the same thing to me all the time.'

'Maybe she's right, though.' Bettina accepted a biscuit and took a bite. 'Maybe this is a stupid thing to do.'

'It's not,' said Michelle firmly.

'It's not,' Peter echoed. 'It's a good idea.'

'But it's not working!'

That was undeniable. Michelle scratched her nose, and Peter began to counsel patience: you couldn't expect miracles immediately. 'If at first you don't succeed, try and try again,' he quoted. 'Maybe we should do it in here, next time. Around the table. What do you think, Allie?'

All eyes turned in my direction. I hesitated, my own gaze travelling up the side of the fridge, across the ceiling, down to the cracked linoleum. I saw a drooping calendar; a damp tea towel; a chipped coffee mug. A tap was dripping into the sink. A power cord was wrapped around with silver duct-tape. The whole room was . . . I don't know. Dingy. Ordinary. Clean, but depressing. And hardly what you'd call a place steeped in colourful history.

'I think, if we're going to do this, we should get Delora to help us,' I sighed. 'It's not going to work, otherwise. It's just not.'

'But you said Delora would charge us!' Michelle objected. 'Forty dollars an hour, you said!'

'Because she's a professional. Because she knows what she's doing.' I looked at Bettina. 'Would your mother have that sort of money? I guess not.'

Bettina shook her head. 'Not to spare,' she replied.

'Well, okay. What about this, then?' Taking a deep breath, I tried to summarise my thoughts on the matter. 'We're starting a club, right? The Exorcists' Club. Now a proper club has not only regular meetings, and a set

49

of rules, and a president, but a treasurer as well. And the treasurer takes care of the club funds. Right?'

There were no disagreements.

'Right,' I continued, pleased with my progress so far. 'Then what if we agree to do some fundraising in the future – like baking cakes, or something; we'll work that out – and in the meantime we each donate a portion of our pocket-money savings? Like ten dollars each, say. What about that? Does everyone agree with that?' Seeing pursed lips and raised eyebrows, I added: 'We've got to have some kind of policy on people with no money. If we only do things for people with money, we might never do anything at all.'

Slowly, Michelle nodded. 'That's a good point,' she said. Peter pulled at his bottom lip. Bettina cleared her throat. 'You want me to pay, too?' she asked.

'Of course,' I told her.

'But I'm not a member of the Exorcists' Club. Am I?'

'Of course you are.' Again I sought Michelle's agreement, with an inquiring glance; again Michelle nodded.

'That's if you want to be,' she said, glancing at Bettina. 'Do you?'

'Oh, yes! Please!'

'But ten dollars,' Peter protested. 'That's a lot of money.'

I frowned, because although Peter's family is big (he has two brothers and three sisters), he lives in an enormous house with five bedrooms and two bathrooms and a double garage and a grape vine and a special pen for the dogs. But then I saw how his eyes flicked towards Bettina, and realised what he was trying to say.

'Oh,' I muttered. 'Right. Um . . .' I thought about my savings account, which contained sixty-eight dollars and thirty-five cents. I've always been a good saver. And Dad's always sent me money for my birthday. 'Okay, how about this?' I said. 'I'll pay Bettina's share, and she can pay me back some time. Whenever she can. Maybe her mum or her aunt wouldn't mind paying ten dollars for a session with Delora, since Delora's a real professional.'

'I could ask,' Bettina offered timidly. 'I could ask them.'

'Okay. You do that.' Noting her troubled expression, I added: 'If you want, *I* can do it. Since they'll be back here soon.'

I didn't, though, because I didn't have time. Bettina's mum arrived home just ten minutes before Ray knocked on the door. (Thank goodness she *was* there, or Ray would have told Mum that I had been 'unsupervised', and Mum would have been really cross.) Bettina's mother introduced herself as Dubravka. She was lugging a couple of shopping bags full of food and moved as if her feet were sore.

Something about the distracted way she smiled at us all, and frowned at the mail on the kitchen table, and grunted as she crouched down to stick a tin of olive oil under the sink, made me think twice about bringing up Delora's fee. I decided to wait until the poor, weary woman had at least sat down with a hot cup of tea and kicked her shoes off.

51

Then Ray came, and it was too late.

'What did you say your friend's name was?' Ray asked, when we were waiting at the first set of traffic lights on our way home.

'Bettina Berich,' I said.

'Berich.' Ray pondered this, for a minute. 'Where's it from, do you know? Is it European?'

I shrugged.

'Polish, maybe. Slavic?'

He didn't expect a reply; he was thinking aloud. So I left him to it, and considered the unsuccessful séance. It had been disappointing not to get a result, but also something of a relief. I wasn't at all sure that I could have coped with Michael's ghost. Suppose it had tapped me on the shoulder, or lifted the cap off my head? I would have screamed the place down.

No, on reflection, it would be much more sensible to have Delora taking charge of things. She would know what to do if Michael's moaning, broken-backed spirit suddenly appeared. For one thing, she would probably know how to get rid of it.

As soon as Ray stopped the car, I rushed inside and called Delora. Delora consulted her diary. By dinner time, our next séance had been arranged for Saturday night, with Delora Starburn booked for an appearance.

CHAPTER # five

'What do you mean, you can't make it on Saturday?'
my dad demanded.

'I've got something on.' Because he sounded hurt,
I added: 'Sorry.'

'But I told you Matoaka wanted to cook you dinner!'

'Friday night, you said. You said Friday night.'

'I said Friday *or* Saturday.'

'Well . . .' I didn't know what to say. He seemed
cross, so I didn't want to remind him that he had
used the words 'probably Friday'. 'Can't she do it on
Friday?'

'No. That's the whole point. She has a yoga class.
Damn it.'

There was a long silence on the other end of the
telephone line. I felt a bit guilty.

'Can she do it on Sunday?' I suggested. But Dad didn't seem to hear.

'What's so important on Saturday that you can't come?' he asked. 'A birthday party? It's not something your mum's arranged, is it?'

'No.' I hesitated. 'It's a séance.'

'A *what*?'

'A séance.' I tried to explain. 'We've hired a medium, you see. I have to be there, because, well, because it's important.' I didn't bother telling him that I had been elected President of the Exorcists' Club (at a quick bus-line election meeting), so had a duty to show up at our first proper séance. I didn't think I ought to tell Dad about the Exorcists' Club before I told Mum – and I hadn't told Mum, at that stage.

'You're going to a séance?' he exclaimed. 'Why, for God's sake?'

'Because my friend wants to talk to her cousin. He's dead.'

'I still don't see why that means *you* have to go.'

'I have to. I promised.'

Another long silence. I was using the kitchen phone, but there was nobody else in the kitchen; Mum had taken Bethan to footy practice, and Ray was in his studio out the back, painting.

'Well, I don't know if I approve,' said Dad, at last. 'Séances and that sort of thing would be harmless rubbish, if they didn't involve an obsession with death – and an obsession with death *is* harmful. It creates

54

stagnant energies. Does your mother know about this?'

'Yes,' I replied. In fact, Mum hadn't been very happy either, when I'd first revealed my plans for Saturday night. We had been eating our dinner, and she had knitted her brows when I told her that I needed to go to Bettina's, on Saturday evening, because Delora Starburn would be holding a séance there. Mum didn't know what it would involve, exactly, so she was a bit anxious. But when I'd informed her that Bettina's mother and aunt would be present, she had agreed to let me go – as long as she, too, was allowed to attend.

She's seen Delora at work before, you see. So she knows how weird things can get, when a psychic is called in.

'Mum's going with me,' I assured Dad, who made a funny noise at the other end of the line.

'I knew it,' he said. 'So it was her idea?'

'No. It was my idea.'

'Is she there? Can I talk to her?'

'No. She's out with Bethan.'

'And she's left you there on your *own*?'

'No. Ray's here.'

'Oh.' I think he must have forgotten about Ray. 'Well, get her to call me, will you? When she gets back?'

'All right.' I cleared my throat, and repeated my former suggestion. 'Can Matoaka cook us dinner on Sunday, Dad?'

'I'll ask her.' He sniffed. 'She's doing us both a favour, Alethea, I hope you realise that.'

'Yes. I do.'

'If she can't do it on Sunday, I suppose we'll have to put it off a week. Or Bethan can come by himself. How would you feel about that?'

I was feeling a bit cross, actually – I'm not sure why. But I didn't want to appear impolite, or ungenerous. 'That's fine,' I said.

'Really?'

'Oh, yeah.'

I was expecting that he would approve of my unselfishness, but his voice was cranky when he said goodbye. I thought: Well, you *said* Friday. 'Probably Friday' – that's what you said. And I reflected glumly that this séance business seemed to be creating a lot of friction in the family.

First there had been the discussion with Mum. Then, after she had agreed to let me go to Bettina's – as long as she accompanied me – Bethan had wanted to come with us. When I'd said 'no', Bethan had sulked. Now Dad was sulking. No wonder I had decided to wait before telling Mum about the Exorcists' Club. She was bound to get worried about that, too.

In the end, Matoaka agreed to cook dinner for Bethan and me on Sunday night. Dad rang to tell us this on Friday, and Mum answered the phone. They proceeded to have an enormous argument about the séance, before Mum finally hung up on him. Then, as if I didn't feel guilty enough, Bettina called to tell me that her aunt was determined to pay Delora's entire fee.

'She's so excited,' Bettina faltered. 'So happy, you know? Like – going around singing. I almost wish . . .' A pause. 'I almost wish we hadn't started this. Because what happens if it doesn't work? She'll be very disappointed. *Very* disappointed.'

'Did you warn her, though? Did you warn her it might not work?'

'Oh, yes. But she thinks, because it costs forty dollars, it will work.' Bettina sighed. 'My mother's not pleased, because Auntie doesn't earn much money, and she always spends it on silly things like huge, enormous bunches of flowers for Michael's grave, and this is another waste of money. My mum thinks.'

'Oh.' That didn't sound good. 'Is your mum very mad?'

'No, not really.' Another sigh. 'Just worried. Worried about my auntie.'

I was worried, too. But I had to *stop* worrying, because my research had cautioned me against it. Worried people, the books had said, could ruin a séance.

That's why I wasn't sure that my own mother should be attending. On the way to Bettina's house, Mum kept asking questions. Why had I got involved in this business? Was Bettina's house haunted? What was Delora's view on our chances – did she think that my friend's cousin would really be accessible?

'I don't know how much use this is going to be,' she fretted. 'I don't know if it's a healthy way of dealing with grief, I really don't.'

'That's what Dad said,' I remarked, and Mum's head whipped around.

'What?'

'That's what Dad said. When I told him. He said it wasn't healthy.'

Mum snorted. '*He* should talk,' she growled, but wouldn't explain further. We reached Bettina's house just after six. I knocked on the front door, which Bettina opened. She smiled at me anxiously.

'You're the first,' she said. 'Come in.'

Behind Bettina stood her aunt, dressed in black, with a reddish tint in her dark hair. There was some confusion, at first, because Bettina's aunt was under the impression that my mum was really Delora. Bettina had to sort that out before we could introduce ourselves properly.

In fact there was quite a lot of confusion, because Bettina had to keep explaining things to Astra in Croatian. (Croatia is where Bettina's family originally came from, I found out.) Bettina's mum spoke better English than her sister did, but was a lot less chatty than Astra, remaining in the kitchen while Astra fluttered around the living room. I sensed that Bettina's mum was displeased about something, though she served up coffee, cake and lemon drink politely enough. It was Bettina herself who alerted me to her mother's state of mind, because she was always glancing nervously at Mrs Berich, and offering to help with the washing-up, or make the coffee, or wipe down the table, or answer the phone.

'No, no,' Bettina's mother would say. 'You look after your guests. They are your guests, Bettina.'

Josie wasn't around. I decided that she was probably out at the movies with her friends, or something. She wasn't the sort of teenager you'd expect to see hanging around the house on a Saturday night.

'My oldest daughter is at a party,' Bettina's mum explained, when my mum commented on the big photograph in the living room. 'She goes to a lot of parties, but what can you do? You can't lock them inside.'

'That is Michael,' Astra said eagerly, pointing at the only male in the picture. 'My son, Michael. He was seventeen years old.'

'Oh.' My mum cleared her throat, uneasily. I had told her about Michael. 'I'm so sorry. I was so sorry to hear.'

'Maybe he is with his father,' Astra continued. Her voice was pretty, but her face was worn, and full of dark lines. She was much thinner than her sister. 'I want to talk to him. Find out . . .'

'Yes, of course.' Mum already looked upset, because Astra's eyes were bright with tears. 'I understand.'

Then Michelle arrived, with Peter. (I guess Michelle's mum must have picked him up.) Michelle was dressed in one of the fancy outfits that her mother is always buying her: a kind of furry jacket thing over copper-coloured pants, with gold earrings. She had brought a tin of Italian chocolate wafers.

Peter had brought nothing but his backpack, which he pretty much takes everywhere. It's usually full of books and computer games.

'So everyone's here except Delora, is that right?' Mum queried, accepting a cup of coffee. I hoped very much that she had noticed the absence of any *other* parents at this gathering – except, of course, for the parents who actually lived in Bettina's house. Then it occurred to me that neither Michelle's mum nor Peter's mum probably believed in the paranormal, so they wouldn't have been worried. Not like my own mum. She's seen what ghosts can do.

Perhaps Michelle was so keen about the Exorcists' Club, and summoning up spirits, because she *hasn't* seen what ghosts can do. Not really. I'm the only one in the club who's actually had to live in a haunted house.

'We probably ought to go to the toilet before Delora arrives,' I suggested. 'Just in case we have to sit still for a long time.'

'That's a good idea,' said Mum, and we all took it in turns to empty our bladders. By the time we'd finished, Delora was teetering down the driveway on very high heels. Bettina spotted her through the living-room window, and rushed to let her in. As soon as the front door opened, the smell of Delora's perfume swirled into the house.

'Hello, sweetie. Oh – you're Bettina, are you? Allie told me about you. Hello Judy – Allie, darl – ah!

Now, I remember you two, but I can't remember your names . . .'

'Michelle.'

'Peter.'

'Michelle and Peter, *that's* right.' Delora beamed at my friends. She was wearing a lacy, see-through shirt over a pink lycra tank top, and stretch jeans trimmed with lace on the cuffs and pockets. Her hair was blonde again (it had been reddish, at one stage), except where there were dark bits showing at the roots. Her false fingernails were a silvery colour, and her lipstick was purple.

Bettina's mum, who had emerged from the kitchen, said something in Croatian to her stunned-looking sister. Her sister stammered something back.

Delora smiled at both of them, revealing teeth stained yellow by cigarettes.

'Delora Starburn,' she supplied. 'How do you do?'

'My sister is the one you want to talk to,' Bettina's mum said, gesturing. 'I am not involved.'

And don't want to be, her tone seemed to imply.

Delora studied her intently for a moment, a smile still plastered across her tanned face.

'But you intend to stay in the house?' she asked Mrs Berich.

'Of course.'

'Then if you *don't* mind, sweetie, I need you out of the room where we'll be engaged. Nothing personal, but you're going to disrupt things, otherwise.'

61

Bettina's mum snorted, and withdrew. Delora turned to Astra, who was still looking dazed.

'Astra, is it? Good. And you're the bereaved in this case, are you?'

It's always surprised me that Delora can't tell these things at a glance, being psychic. Astra was wearing black, after all. But then again, so was her sister.

'My aunt wants to speak to her son,' Bettina announced. 'Her son was Michael. That's his picture.'

'Ah.' Delora studied it. 'What a lovely boy, Astra, I'm *so* sorry.'

'Yes,' said Astra. 'He was my lovely son.'

'And do you have anything personal of his? Something he used to wear, perhaps?'

'The hat,' I broke in. 'The baseball cap. Over there.'

'Lovely,' said Delora. She picked up the cap, glancing around the room as she did so. 'Are we going to sit in here?' she inquired. 'We'll need a few chairs, and a table.'

'There's a table in the kitchen,' said Bettina. 'We can sit in the kitchen.'

'All right, then. Lead the way.'

We all trooped into the kitchen. It smelled spicy, as if someone had recently been cooking. Freshly washed dishes were piled up on the draining board. It looked less dreary at night than it did during the day.

'How many people?' Delora wondered, and began to count. 'One, two, three, four . . . seven. We'll need one extra chair.'

'I'll get it,' said Bettina, scooting out.

'Now, Astra,' Delora went on, 'I have to warn you that this might not work. Do you understand? Sometimes the spirits just aren't accessible.' Seeing Astra's blank expression, Delora began to speak more slowly and deliberately. 'Sometimes, when people die, their spirits don't remain within reach of this world,' she explained. 'And that's generally a *good* thing, because when there's still a connection, it means that the deceased is not at peace. If we *do* manage to contact your son, it's because he's been held to this reality by some sense of disquiet, some feeling that he's left something unfinished or unsaid. Do you understand?'

It didn't appear so. Astra was frowning, concentrating fiercely, but she still looked confused. Then Bettina returned, with an old cane-bottomed chair, and Delora had to repeat herself, after which Bettina was able to translate everything for her aunt's benefit.

'Okay,' said Delora finally, satisfied that Astra's enthusiastic nod signified understanding. 'Let's all sit down, and join hands, and touch feet. Michelle, sweetie, would you turn off the light for me? *That's* a good girl.' With the light off, it was quite dark, though a faint glow still filtered through from the living room, where Mrs Berich was moving around.

There was a clicking noise, and the sound of gunfire.

'Oh, Mrs Berich?' Delora pleaded, raising her voice. 'Could you not watch the television, please? It's very distracting.'

63

Astra suddenly called out sharply, in Croatian, and the television clicked off again. Heavy footsteps faded down the hallway. A door slammed.

'My sister does not believe,' Astra remarked apologetically.

'That's all right,' Delora responded. 'As long as she keeps out of the way. Now. I want you next to me, Astra, and . . . let's see, now.' Her thoughtful gaze travelled from me to Bettina, and back again. 'And Allie, I think. Yes, Allie on my other side. Right here, Allie.'

I wondered why I had been chosen to hold Delora's hand. My 'dark aura', perhaps? Sitting close to Delora, I could smell smoke on her breath, and realised with a start that she hadn't lit a cigarette since her arrival.

Maybe she didn't smoke while she was 'channelling'.

'All right,' she sighed, when we were all in our chairs. 'Everyone comfortable? Yes? Then I want you all to close your eyes. Those of you who knew Michael, I want you to think about him. Those of you who didn't, I want you to focus on the hands that you're holding. Just that.'

'Don't we have to sing?' Peter piped up. 'Sing and recite prayers?'

'Well, if you want to.' Delora didn't sound fussed, one way or another. 'I've never really found it necessary, though if you have that wonderful CD, Astra – that one with Gregorian chants on – that's a terrific conduit.'

'We don't have any chants,' Bettina apologised, answering for her aunt. 'Just pop music.'

64

'Then there's not much point,' said Delora. 'Unless you all know one song that you can sing. If you're all concentrating on one song, it will transform your breathing and focus your energies. But only if you all know one song.'

We didn't. At least, we couldn't think of any – not that Astra knew. She wasn't even familiar with 'Silent night', or 'Waltzing Matilda', or 'Row, row, row your boat'. So we scrapped the idea of a song.

Instead we just sat there in silence, concentrating on our neighbours' hands. I was holding Mum's hand on one side, and Delora's on the other. Mum's hand was fidgety, but Delora's was odd. Really odd. At first, it was perfectly relaxed, so relaxed that it almost seemed boneless. It wasn't sweating or twitching or even pulsing with the flow of her blood. It just hung there limply, and would have slid out of my grasp if I hadn't applied any pressure.

Then gradually, after what seemed a very long while, I became aware that Delora's hand was beginning to vibrate. The sensation was so peculiar that I opened my eyes and glanced at Delora, and gasped. She looked awful. She looked *dead*. Her mouth hung ajar, her head had rolled to one side, her eyelids were partly open, displaying only the whites of her eyes.

When Michelle squeaked, I realised that she, too, must be looking at Delora.

'Oh, my God,' Mum breathed, and leaned forward. I immediately jerked her back.

'No!' I hissed. 'You mustn't interfere! It's dangerous!' I remembered having read about that in a book. 'Don't ever grab a medium, or you might stop her from returning to consciousness!'

Suddenly Delora shuddered; I could feel the force of it right up my own arm. A weird sound issued from her throat – a kind of rattling sound. Everybody at the table jumped.

Delora started panting harshly.

'Michael!' Astra cried, in a high, urgent voice, and let fall a string of Croatian words. She was gazing around wildly, as if hoping to catch a glimpse of her dead son. Bettina was whimpering. The panting continued.

A loud *crack* nearly gave me a heart attack.

'What was that?' Mum demanded.

'Shh! *Mum!*'

'It's like something broke,' Peter whispered uneasily. Delora had slumped forward. Her hand gave a shudder as her body convulsed. By this time, I have to admit, I was *terrified*. I thought she was having a fit, or something.

Astra began to cry.

'Michael,' she sobbed. 'Michael!'

My feet were getting cold.

CHAPTER # six

Then, quite abruptly, it was all over.

Delora uttered a great, cawing gasp, and threw herself backwards, releasing my hand. She coughed and coughed. Finally she looked up, chest heaving, eyes streaming, and groaned.

'Delora?' said Mum. 'Are you all right?'

Delora nodded. She was coughing again.

'Are we finished?' asked Peter, in bewilderment. But no one answered.

'Ohh,' said Delora. '*Oh*, dear. *Oh*, my.' Her voice was very hoarse. 'Could I have a glass of water?'

Bettina got up, went to the tap, and filled a coffee cup with water. Meanwhile, Delora looked around the table.

'What happened?' she rasped.

Heads turned as we all exchanged glances.

'What do you mean?' said Mum. 'Don't you remember?'

'No. Never do.'

'You *never* do?'

'No.' Delora sounded a little cross. 'I told you that before, didn't I?' She accepted the cup of water with a murmur of thanks, and drained it in four swallows as we all watched her. At last she lowered her head and wiped her mouth, smearing lipstick all over the place. 'So,' she went on, blinking wearily. 'Did we get anything? Anything at all?'

'Uh . . .' No one wanted to tell her. Once more, we all looked at each other.

'There was a noise,' Peter said at last. 'Sort of a cracking noise. Like something broke.'

'*Did* anything break?' asked Delora.

'I don't think so.'

'This house makes a lot of funny noises,' Bettina offered. 'It's always creaking and banging.'

'Anything else?' Delora was rubbing her eyes. 'Did I say anything?'

'No.'

'Not really.'

'You just sort of grunted.'

Delora checked her watch. So did I. It was ten to seven.

'Mmmph,' she said. 'Not very long.'

'Where is Michael?' Astra suddenly demanded. She was glaring at Delora. 'Where is my son?'

'Ah.' Delora looked very tired. 'Your son. Yes. Well, I don't know, sweetie, I'm sorry. I don't know where he is. Except that he's not here.'

'Eh?' said Astra, and turned to her niece. They swapped a few Croatian remarks, at which Astra flushed. She spluttered and scowled.

'What?' she exclaimed, rounding on Delora. 'You must speak to him! Now!'

'I can't,' Delora replied. 'I'm truly sorry.'

'But you *said*!'

'I said it might not work,' Delora pointed out. 'I did warn you.'

'I want to talk to my son!'

'I know. I understand. But your son is no longer here, sweetie. He's gone. He's at peace. It's a good thing.'

'No!'

'Yes.'

Astra screeched something at her niece, who coloured and said, in a very soft voice: 'Could you try again, please? My aunt wants you to try again.'

'I can't.' Delora's own voice was flat and exhausted. She began to rise from the chair, her joints cracking. 'I opened a channel, and nothing came through. It wears me out. I can't do it again tonight, and I doubt there'd be any point if I could. He's obviously not around.'

Whatever Astra said next upset Bettina quite a lot. The two of them began to argue. Michelle leant over and pulled at my sleeve.

'What about that, eh?' she murmured, bright-eyed. 'Wasn't that spooky?'

'I guess.'

'Did you feel it getting cold? I could feel it getting cold.'

'Don't be stupid!' Bettina cried, breaking into English. She was addressing her aunt, but threw an agonised glance at me, adding: 'She doesn't want to . . . you know . . .' And she rubbed her right thumb and fore-finger together.

Clearly, Astra didn't want to pay.

'Oh,' I said. 'Right. Um . . .' Thinking quickly, I realised that this wouldn't be a problem – we would simply return to our original plan. The difficulty was that I didn't have the money on me. Neither, I was sure, did Michelle or Peter. Would Delora take an IOU? Or would I have to ask Mum to write a cheque, and pay her back later? I wasn't too happy about appealing to Mum. And I didn't know if Delora would be charging us the full fee; after all, she had only been at the house for a little over half an hour. 'Delora,' I began, 'could you just come in here, for a second? I have to ask you something. In private. It's okay, Mum, it's nothing bad.'

I don't know why I took Delora into Bettina's room. Probably because I wasn't too familiar with the rest of the house, except the bathroom, and Bettina's mum was in there. I didn't turn the light on, because I didn't really need to; light was already filtering in from the hallway, and through the slats of Bettina's venetian blinds. She had left some dirty socks on the floor, and a squashed school hat on the bed. When I walked through the door, I stepped on a crisp packet.

'The thing is,' I began, ushering Delora over the threshold and speaking very quietly, 'I was wondering about the money. Because originally Astra was going to pay, but now she isn't, which is okay because we have enough, only I was wondering if we could pay you tomorrow, or whether you'd want a cheque from my mum . . . Delora? Are you all right?'

She was blinking and grimacing, shaking her head from side to side as if she had an earache. She put a hand to her head. She staggered backwards, wobbling on her high heels.

'What is it?' I said. 'Are you sick?'

'Oh, my God,' she gasped, screwing up her eyes.

'Delora?'

But she had stumbled out of the room. I followed her anxiously, and saw how she had to prop herself against the walls of the corridor. Only when she reached the kitchen did she stop, framed in the doorway, kneading her temples with both hands.

'God,' she groaned. 'Who sleeps in there?'

'What?' said Mum. Everyone else just stared.

'In that room? The little one?' Delora squinted around at a circle of blank faces. 'Does somebody actually *sleep* in there?'

Seeing that no one had the faintest idea what she

was talking about, I spoke up myself. 'Bettina does,' I said.

'Well, she shouldn't,' Delora snapped. 'She should stay out of it. Everybody should. That's a black hole, in there.'

'What do you mean?' It was Peter who spoke, because Bettina seemed to have been struck dumb. 'What do you mean, a black hole?'

'That room! It's practically howling! Have you been in there? Have you felt it?' Delora looked at me. '*You* must have felt something, Allie, I can't believe *no one's* noticed anything. I haven't felt an energy like that in years!'

Flattered, I tried to interpret what she was saying.

'You mean – there's some sort of psychic energy in there?' I said, drawing on my mum's endless lectures about Feng Shui. 'Like negative *chi*, or something?'

'I don't know about negative *chi*,' Delora replied, closing her eyes as she massaged her temples, 'but that room is voracious. It's crying out. It's *hungry*. Haven't you picked up on that?' She shuddered. Then one blue eye flicked open, and was trained on Bettina. 'Haven't you noticed the *hunger* in that room?'

Although Bettina's mouth opened, no sound emerged. Astra jabbed at her arm, crossly addressing her in Croatian. Bettina didn't respond.

'*I* noticed the hunger,' Michelle suddenly announced, her breath quickening, her eyes widening. 'Allie! Don't you remember? Don't you remember how hungry we got, last time we were here?'

I was startled.

'Oh, but that was after school,' I objected. 'Every-one's always hungry after school.'

'I'm not,' Michelle retorted. 'Not that hungry. Not right after school.'

'But –'

'Could it make us hungry? That room?' Michelle interrupted, her attention switching to Delora. 'We were in there for nearly an hour, and we were all starv-ing when we came out. We ate and ate.'

'Did you?' Delora seemed to perk up. 'Really? Well, that *is* interesting. Yes, that would make sense. I can see that might happen.'

'Wow,' said Michelle. Bettina gaped. Peter was frowning.

'Wait,' he said. 'Wait a minute. Are you saying that there's a strange energy in that room, and it makes everyone who goes in really hungry?'

'Could do,' Delora replied. She looked at Bettina, shaking her head in amazement. 'It's incredible that you can actually sleep there. *I* couldn't,' she said.

It crossed my mind that the hungry energy might be coming from Bettina – who obviously ate a lot – but I didn't say anything. I didn't know how to, without upsetting Bettina. It was Peter who worked out what question to ask.

'So would the energy come from someone who's alive, or someone who's dead?' he inquired carefully.

'Oh, dead,' Delora replied. She was scooping up her handbag. 'No question. Dead quite recently, I'd say, or the vibrations wouldn't be so strong. Within the last five years, at a guess.'

By now Astra was shaking her niece's arm, speaking very sharply. Mum was trying to calm her down. Then Delora (who was looking a little frayed around the edges) informed me that she would send me an invoice; we would sort out the money question later. 'I've got a shocking headache,' she declared. 'Time for a cup of tea and an aspirin, I think. Goodbye, Astra. Judy. So sorry it didn't work out. Bettina, darl . . .' She raised her voice, fixing Bettina with a stern look. 'You shouldn't be sleeping in that bedroom. It can't be doing you any good, sweetie, you should ask your mum to move you.'

Bettina blinked. 'Me?' she said faintly. 'Move?'

'Can't she just get rid of the energy?' Michelle piped up, and Delora shrugged.

'She can try. *I* could try, if you want, though I don't know if I'd be much help.' Seeing my puzzled expression, Delora slung her bag over her shoulder, and struggled to explain. 'That's a very primitive hunger, in that room,' she went on. 'It's strong, so I could tell at once – it has no subtleties, no complications, it's just a yawning *hole*. It's not going to tell me anything, not even if I connect, which is something I'd rather not do, if you don't mind.' She shuddered. 'A force like that could cause a lot of damage.'

'So what do you suggest?' Peter frowned. 'A séance? In the bedroom?'

74

'We've already done that,' I objected. 'Nothing happened except that we all felt hungry.'

'Which is what I was talking about.' Delora moved towards the front door. 'It's so fundamental, it's a dead end. No – Bettina should move. She should sleep somewhere else.'

'But there's nowhere else *to* sleep!' Bettina cried.

Delora, however, didn't seem to hear. She was already disappearing into the night, her high heels clacking on cement. Normally, she isn't so rude; she likes to talk, and will stand around chatting all day if you let her. I decided that the force in Bettina's room had shaken her badly.

She was scampering out of there as fast as her legs could carry her.

'Okay,' said Peter, quietly. He was standing beside me, I realised, with Michelle hovering at his elbow. Mum and Astra had remained a few paces behind, and were struggling to communicate; Mum was trying to explain that Michael was at peace, unreachable, while Astra muttered darkly about broken promises, clutching her niece's arm.

'Okay, what's the plan?' Peter wanted to know. 'There's obviously a ghost in Bettina's bedroom. How do we get rid of it?'

'Oh!' Michelle sounded surprised. 'Is *that* what Delora was saying? I thought she was talking about a force, not a ghost.'

'Same thing,' Peter replied impatiently. 'It's like Eglantine all over again, except this ghost doesn't write messages. This ghost isn't smart enough. It's *primitive*, Delora said. Primitive.'

'Like an animal?' I hazarded. 'A dog, or something?'

'A hungry dog!' Michelle supplied. 'A dead, hungry dog.'

'Which died in Bettina's bedroom,' Peter finished. He tapped his front teeth, pondering. 'Maybe someone went on holiday, and left their dog locked in the house, and it died.'

'Like those dogs that get locked in cars,' Michelle said solemnly.

We all looked towards the bedrooms, just as Bettina's mum emerged, her hair still damp from a recent shower. She glanced around, and said something in Croatian.

'She's gone,' Bettina replied in shrill tones. 'Delora's gone. It didn't work. She said it might not work.'

Bettina's mum snorted. She turned to her sister and plunged into a conversation that I didn't understand. Peter and I exchanged glances.

'I'm sorry,' Bettina murmured, approaching us both as her aunt released her. She was blinking back tears. 'This is so embarrassing.'

'It doesn't matter.' I wished that Bettina wouldn't always take things so hard. 'We agreed that we'd split the fee, right at the beginning.'

'I warned her,' Bettina continued fretfully. 'I warned her over and over again not to expect anything, but she wouldn't listen. I *told* her it didn't always work.'

I shrugged, and Peter tugged at his bottom lip.

Michelle said, 'What do you mean? Of course it worked. We didn't talk to Michael, Bettina, but we found out why you've been putting on weight. You've got a Hungry Energy in your bedroom.'

I couldn't help wincing. Peter did the same. There's no way in the world I would have mentioned Bettina's weight, not like that. Sometimes I can't believe the way Michelle comes right out and says things about amputated arms or Downs Syndrome kids or muttering old men without shoes on, discussing them so matter-of-factly, so coolly, as if it were the most natural thing in the world. She seems surprised when I can't do the same. Too self-conscious, I guess.

Michelle is hardly ever self-conscious. It's one of the things I like about her.

'Well, it's true, isn't it?' she queried, glancing from face to face. 'Obviously Bettina's been eating too much because her bedroom's making her feel hungry all the time.'

I didn't know what to say. Agreeing would make it look as if I thought Bettina was fat. To my surprise, however, Bettina herself didn't seem offended.

'Do you think so?' she asked Michelle. 'Do you think that's the problem?'

'Don't *you*?' Michelle retorted.

'I guess . . .'

'It seems to me,' said Michelle, 'that you should either start sleeping somewhere else, or we should get rid of this ghost. Don't you agree, Allie?'

I did. It was the obvious conclusion to draw. The trouble was, I didn't know where to start when it came to exorcising the ghost in Bettina's bedroom.

And I couldn't think, because Mum was calling to me.

'Allie!' she exclaimed. 'Come on, please, we're going.'

'But, Mum –'

'Say goodbye to Mrs Berich. She's put up with us for long enough.'

'Can I just – I have to go to the toilet.' And I needed a moment's peace. 'Mum? Can I just go to the toilet?'

'All right, but hurry, please.'

The bathroom smelled of hot soap. Every surface was covered with a film of condensation from Mrs Berich's shower; I had to wipe the toilet seat before I could sit down on it. Then I considered our options. Delora had said that the ghost couldn't have been dead long. Perhaps some of Bettina's neighbours might remember the people who had lived in the house before. Some might even remember if a dog had died in one of these rooms.

When tracking down Eglantine, I had asked Mum to get a copy of the title deeds to our house, which told you the names of everyone who had ever owned it back to the late nineteenth century. Would Mrs Berich be able to dig up the title deeds to *her* house? It would be a start, I thought. It would give us a name, at least. But when I returned to the living room, and asked Mrs Berich about title deeds, she just stared at me blankly.

'Mrs Berich doesn't own this house, Allie,' my mother hastened to explain. 'I'm sorry, Dubravka, she's a funny little thing. Allie, Mrs Berich rents this house. She wouldn't have access to any title deeds.'

'Who would, then?' I requested. 'Who owns the house?'

'Now come on, Allie, that's enough, we have to go.'

'Inner West Community Housing,' Bettina suddenly declared. 'They own it.'

'Would they know who used to live here?' I was being hustled towards the front door, but kept talking to Bettina anyway. 'They might, don't you think? It's worth a try. We have to find out who used to live here.'

'We could ask the neighbours,' Peter suggested, following me. 'Bettina could ask the neighbours.'

'Yes,' I agreed. 'That would be good. All *right*, Mum, I'm coming.' By this time we were marching up the driveway. 'Could you ask the neighbours, Bettina? And I'll phone this Inner West Housing place.'

'Inner West *Community* Housing,' Bettina corrected anxiously. It was so dark outside that I couldn't see her face very well, but she didn't sound too keen. 'I – I don't really know the neighbours,' she stammered. 'We've only been here a few months.'

'They seem all right though, don't they?' As Mum unlocked our car, I grabbed the handle on the front passenger door. 'It'll be a chance for you to meet them. Just ask them if anything – or anyone – died in your house.'

'Wait a minute.' Though eager to make her escape, Mum was also concerned about my friends. She paused with one foot in the car. 'How are you getting home, Michelle? Is your mother picking you up?'

'I'm supposed to ring her.'

'Do you want a lift? Peter? Would you both like a lift?'

In the end, Mum gave Peter and Michelle a lift home. It wasn't a very long ride. Even so, we managed to discuss our next move during the few minutes it took to reach Peter's place, agreeing that I should call Inner West Community Housing on Monday. Meanwhile, on Sunday, Bettina would make inquiries around her neighbourhood.

'There's bound to be someone who remembers,' I insisted, 'especially if someone – or something – died in that house. Delora said it must have happened recently. Someone *has* to remember.'

'Unless it was a dog or a cat,' said Michelle. 'Lots of people don't care about animals.'

'Kids would know,' said Peter. 'Kids notice animals.' And then Mum spoke up.

'I hope you kids aren't expecting Bettina to go door-knocking all on her own,' she objected. 'You must realise that's not safe.'

I looked at Peter. Michelle looked at me.

'I wouldn't let any child of mine go door-knocking unless she had at least two friends with her,' Mum continued, in forbidding tones. She pulled into Peter's driveway. 'All right. Here we are. Now.' She turned in her seat. 'What's going on? Hmm? I don't like all this messing about with the supernatural, it's not safe. Especially when it comes to door-knocking.'

'Oh, it's okay, Mum,' I interrupted quickly. 'I'll go with Bettina tomorrow.'

'And me,' Peter chimed in.

'I can't,' complained Michelle. 'Mum and I are supposed to be visiting Palm Beach, tomorrow.'

'Well, good,' said Mum. 'But you still haven't answered my question. What's going on? I've never met Bettina before, and suddenly you're inviting Delora into her house, and asking about title deeds.' She fixed me with a stern look. 'Allie, you're not pretending to be a PRISM person, are you? You haven't been chasing ghosts?'

'No, not exactly.' I wondered how I could introduce the subject of the Exorcists' Club without alarming my mother. 'Bettina just asked us to help her, because we know about ghosts. She wanted to summon up her cousin's spirit. We didn't know there was *already* a ghost in the house.'

'And we have to get rid of it, Mrs Gebhardt,' Michelle said eagerly. 'I mean, poor Bettina! Imagine how much happier she'll be if we get rid of this ghost, and she loses weight!'

Mum was torn; I could tell. She's not like other mothers. Other mothers would have dismissed the whole business as a big pile of steaming nonsense, and would have let us muck about playing silly 'ghost

81

games' to our hearts' content. Mum, however, believes in ghosts. She doesn't have a choice – not after our encounter with Eglantine. And, while on the one hand she would prefer it if I never again had anything to do with the paranormal, she's also lived in a haunted house, and knows how awful it can be. So she couldn't help sympathising with Bettina.

'Maybe I'd better call PRISM,' she fretted. 'Maybe they can help.'

'They didn't help *us*, Mum,' I pointed out.

'Yes, but –'

'We'll just be doing research,' I said. 'Like we did with Eglantine. Maybe, if we work out who this ghost is, and what it wants, we can make sure it's satisfied and send it away. Ghosts,' I added, 'are always hanging around because they want something. We know *that* by now. Don't we?'

When Mum sighed, I knew I'd won.

CHAPTER # seven

The next day, when I arrived at the Beriches' house, Bettina had some exciting news.

'Guess what happened?' she exclaimed, as soon as she had opened the front door. I waved to Ray (who was pulling away from the kerb), and he beeped his horn. Then I turned back to Bettina.

'What?' I said.

'Josie slept in my room last night, and she ate all the cheesecake!' Bettina's eyes were as round as marbles; her voice was breathless. Ushering me into the living room, she informed me that Peter wasn't there, yet. 'I didn't want to sleep in my room again,' she went on, her words tumbling out, 'and I told Josie why, and she said I was stupid, and she said she would prove there was nothing wrong with my room. So we swapped beds, and this morning the cheesecake was gone! And the olives, too! And the almonds!'

'So, hang on.' There was too much information. I couldn't absorb it all. 'Are you saying Josie got up in the middle of the night and ate a whole cheesecake?'

'Half a cheesecake. And a whole jar of olives, and a packet of almonds.'

'Has she ever done it before?'

'No!' Bettina said triumphantly. 'It's what *I* used to do!'

'Really?' I studied her with interest, and she flushed. 'In the middle of the night?'

'I couldn't help it,' she mumbled. 'I was so hungry.'

Then a knock on the door announced Peter's arrival, and Bettina had to tell her story all over again. This time, she also described how Josie had tried to pretend that Bettina was the culprit, until her mum found crumbs in the bed that was usually occupied by Bettina. 'And Josie couldn't pretend that *I'd* dropped them,' Bettina crowed, 'because the sheets were changed last night. She said she wouldn't sleep on *my* smelly old sheets. She had to have her own.'

'So in other words, this is proof that your room makes you hungry,' said Peter.

'Yes! That's right!' Bettina beamed. She was heading into the kitchen, where her mother was washing lunch dishes. 'It's not my fault after all, is it, Mum?'

Mrs Berich looked up from the sink. Her hair hung

in wisps around her face, and there were dark circles under her eyes.

'Hello,' she grunted, nodding at me, then at Peter.

'Hello, Mrs Berich,' we replied.

'It's not my fault, is it Mum?' Bettina pressed. 'It was the room that made me greedy.'

'Perhaps.'

'It *was*! You *said*!'

'I said I'll try it myself tonight,' Mrs Berich retorted. 'See if I get hungry.'

'You will,' said Bettina, in accusing accents. 'Everyone does.'

'Maybe.'

Peter cleared his throat.

'We think there might be a ghost in the room,' he announced. 'Perhaps even the ghost of a hungry dog.'

Scrubbing furiously at a baking pan, Mrs Berich rolled her eyes.

'It's true, Mum!' Bettina blurted out. 'Peter and Allie know about ghosts! They've seen them before!'

'We can't be sure what this is, until we do some research,' I admitted, cautiously, 'but it could be an animal. That's why it's probably worthwhile putting out a bowl of dog food. Just in case the spirit wants something to eat. I mean, it can't hurt.'

Mrs Berich put down her pot scrubber. She turned to look at me, placing a wet, red hand on her hip.

'You think Bettina's room is haunted?' she queried.

'Maybe.' I didn't want to be too definite.

'By a dog?'

'Well, it's one possibility.'

'By a hungry dog,' Peter interjected. 'Delora was saying that the energy in that room is very primitive. So it could be an animal. And if it's hungry, it will want to be fed.'

Mrs Berich cocked her head, a wry expression on her face. 'But dogs like cake,' she objected. 'They like chips and sausage rolls and chocolate biscuits, don't you think?'

Peter and I exchanged glances. 'I – I guess so,' said Peter. 'Some dogs.'

'Well, Bettina is always leaving these things in her room, hidden about the place, and it never seems to make any difference,' Mrs Berich pointed out, causing her daughter to wince and change colour. 'Why should a bowl of dog food satisfy this hungry ghost when the other food does not?'

It was a good point. Peter, however, wouldn't be discouraged.

'Michelle's cat will only eat beef hearts,' he said firmly. 'This dog might only eat dog food.' To my astonishment, he suddenly produced a paper bag from his backpack. 'I brought some dog biscuits with me – we've got plenty, at home. But perhaps we should try cat food, as well.'

I was hugely impressed. How clever he had been, to have thought of dog biscuits!

'Oh, all right,' groaned Mrs Berich. 'I'll do it. I'll buy cat food. Just stop bothering me.'

'Thanks, Mum!'

'But only a little, little tin. The smallest. The cheapest.'

'Okay!'

'And if the ghost doesn't eat it, we can feed it to Josie,' Mrs Berich grumbled, returning to her suds and her pot scrubber. 'She's eaten everything else in this house, today.'

Later, on our way out the door, I congratulated Peter on the dog biscuits. 'It was a smart idea,' I said, wondering why I hadn't thought of it myself. Because of Dad, probably. He was distracting me. I was still turning the whole business over in my head. I was still trying to work out whether Dad would want us to live with him.

I had asked Mum, cautiously, if Dad had mentioned moving. It was the best I could do without alerting her to what I was really worried about. 'No. Why?' was her answer.

'Oh, nothing.'

'I don't think he's going back to Thailand, Allie. Not any time soon.' A penetrating look. 'Is something wrong?'

'No, no.' It hadn't been a lie, either. Not entirely. Nothing was wrong, and nothing would be unless Dad started wanting Bethan and me to live with him.

I didn't want to live with Dad. I didn't even *know* him.

'So where are we going first?' Peter asked. 'Bettina? What do you think?'

We stood at her front gate, glancing from side to

side. Bettina's high spirits seemed to have deserted her. She looked apprehensive.

'I don't know,' she muttered. 'Like I said, we haven't been here long.'

'What about them?' I pointed at the white house to our left, which was bigger than Bettina's, but less tidy. Dead pot plants and dilapidated furniture were strewn across the front yard. A torn and faded awning flapped over one window. Someone had painted half a wall, then stopped; dry paint tins were piled near a ladder. 'There's a bike over there, look. They might have kids.'

'They do,' Bettina conceded. 'Boys.'

'Let's start with them.'

So we trotted over to number twenty-nine, with Bettina bringing up the rear. As soon as I pushed open the squeaky front gate, a very small dog began to bark hysterically from somewhere behind a big stack of cardboard boxes. I could tell it was small, because its voice was so high. Even so, I hesitated.

'It's locked up,' Bettina reassured me. 'Don't worry, they keep it locked up.'

'All day?'

'And all night.' Her tone was grim. 'That's why it's so noisy.'

I wondered if the former occupants of her own house had done the same thing with *their* dog. Cautiously I advanced down the front path, which was littered with lolly wrappers and cigarette butts. The grass looked pretty sick, I thought. The stuffing was

coming out of a big orange couch on the shady verandah, but the rollerblades sitting by the door looked
brand new, and very snazzy.

I knocked, before noticing that there was a doorbell.

'Try the buzzer,' Peter advised, so I did. It was a bell,
not a buzzer; the chimes were faintly audible. After a
minute or so, I heard footsteps. Someone fumbled with
a deadlock on the other side of the door.

Suddenly I was looking at a sour-faced high-school
kid in an oversized T-shirt.

'Oh, hi,' I said. 'Sorry to bother you. We just wanted
to ask about next door – your former next-door neighbours. Did you know them?'

The kid immediately turned on his heel. '*Mum!*' he
yelled, and retreated into the shadows of the hall. I
suppose it was a bit much to expect that any teenage
boy wearing a rude T-shirt and a black woollen beanie
rolled down to his nose would take time to converse
with a twelve-year-old girl.

From somewhere at the back of the house, I could
hear a baby crying.

'They've got a toddler, as well,' Bettina offered. 'Two
big boys and a little one. They fight a lot.'

'Do you hear them from your place?' asked Peter.

'All the time. Especially the boys.'

'Our neighbours are like that too,' said Peter
gloomily. 'Once they cracked their kitchen window
with a dumbbell.'

The *flap-flap-flap* of rubber thongs alerted me to someone's approach. I stepped back as the screen door was pushed open by a woman in grey trackies and a red cardigan. She had lots of curly brown hair, but that was the only perky thing about her. All the rest sagged and drooped.

'What is it?' she snapped. 'We're not buying anything.'

'We're not selling anything,' Peter replied. 'We want to ask about next door.'

'This is Bettina Berich,' I added, pointing. 'She lives next door. She was wondering if you knew anything about the people who used to live there.'

'Next door?' said the woman, frowning. She squinted at Bettina. 'You live in number twenty-seven?'

Bettina nodded, clearly too nervous to speak.

'Then you can tell that other girl to stop shooting her dirty mouth off at my boys!' the woman growled. Before we could do anything but gape at her, she turned on her heel and slammed the door in our faces.

It was quite a shock.

'What a miserable old cow,' Peter grumbled, as we hastily withdrew. 'People always think they can be as rude as they like to children.'

'What did she mean?' I asked Bettina. 'Has Josie been swearing at the boys who live here?'

'Probably.' Bettina sounded resigned. 'Like I said, they make a lot of noise. Especially at night.'

'I bet they aren't even human,' Peter proposed. 'I bet

they're aliens disguised as humans, and they eat their prey at night, after they capture them in alleys and things.'

'Pee-ter,' I groaned.

'You could tell that *she* was an alien,' Peter went on, shooting a vicious look over his shoulder. 'Her skin didn't fit her properly.'

The next house we tried was on the other side of Bettina's place. It was small, and made of bruise-coloured brick. All the paint was peeling off the woodwork, and the windows were shut tight. Behind their dusty panes hung yellowing lace and gauze curtains. The grass needed mowing.

'Are you sure someone lives here?' I asked doubtfully, surveying the secretive facade of the place. 'It doesn't look like it.'

'I've seen a car outside,' Bettina assured me. 'There's a man who visits, and someone always puts out the garbage bin. There's a cat, too.' She indicated a bowl of water near the front steps. 'The cat looks pretty fat, to me.'

'Okay,' I said. 'Here goes.' This time I spotted the doorbell, but it didn't seem to work, because I couldn't hear it chime. No one answered my knock, either.

'I don't think anybody's home,' was Peter's conclusion. 'Either that, or they don't want to talk to us.'

'Let's try across the road,' I suggested.

The house across the road had been fixed up. It had new aluminium windows, a tiled front yard, a satellite dish and a brand new brick fence. The two ladies living there would have helped us, I'm sure, if they had spoken any English. But I think they were both Vietnamese, and we didn't understand each other. The people living next to *them* understood us, but couldn't help. They were two young guys trying to fix a car, and they could tell us only that Bettina's house had changed hands a lot.

'People coming and going,' one of them said. 'Mostly women and their kids.'

'Like the kid with the face,' said the other.

'Oh, yeah. That was bad. Poor kid had a face like it was all mashed up. Couldn't walk, either.'

'Didn't stay long, but.'

'Nup. No one ever does.'

'*We* will,' said Bettina stiffly, but her neighbours just laughed.

'Do you know if any of them had a pet?' I asked. 'A dog or a cat or something? A guinea pig?'

The two men looked at each other. One shrugged. 'Dunno.'

'Never can tell whose dog's barking, round here.'

'Bloody dog across the road never shuts up.'

'Oh, well. Thank you,' said Peter, but I had one more question.

'That house over there,' I remarked, indicating number twenty-five. 'We knocked but nobody answered. Do you know who lives there?'

'Ha!' The bigger guy threw back his head and guffawed. '*Her!*'

'She never comes out,' the other one revealed. 'Too old.'

'Little old lady.'

'Italian. What's her name? Fanciulli?'

'You prob'ly gave her a heart attack.'

'Her son, Livio, he's been trying to sell that house for ages, but she won't leave.'

'You mean she won't come out at *all*?' I exclaimed. '*Ever?*'

'Not since the old man died last year.' The bigger brother wriggled under his car again. 'She's not gunna come out of there till she comes feet first, y'know what I mean?' he finished, his voice sounding muffled.

In that case, I thought, she probably doesn't know much about her next-door neighbours. But when we passed the house again, on our way to Bettina's, I was surprised to see Peter head down Mrs Fanciulli's garden path.

'Where are you going?' I asked him.

'Hang on.'

'What are you doing? Peter?'

By the time I had caught up with him, he was already rapping on the front door. '*Signora!*' he said. '*Scusi, Signora Fanciulli!*'

'What's that you're speaking?' I hissed. 'Peter? What are you up to?'

'Italian,' he replied quietly.

'What?'

'It's Italian. She's Italian. She might not speak anything else.'

I had forgotten that Peter's parents were Italian. It's not something that I normally think about.

'Mind you,' he added, as Bettina joined us, 'she might be from the south. She might only speak some kind of Calabrian dialect, or something, so don't get your hopes up.'

Then he began to spout Italian again; I couldn't tell you what he was saying. It sounded pretty persuasive, though. After about ten minutes, when we were all ready to give up, there was a *click* from behind the door.

Slowly, cautiously, on creaking hinges, it opened a fraction. Hugely enlarged by a very thick pair of spectacles, two watery green eyes peered at us through a narrow crack.

'*Chi siete?*' a quavering voice demanded.

'*Il mio nome é Pietro,*' Peter replied. '*Questa ragazza é* Allie, *é l'altra é* Bettina. Bettina *abita nella casa vicina alla vostra.*'

This, he told me later, was his way of introducing us. He then launched into a long explanation of what we wanted, all in Italian, so Bettina and I could only stand there grinning, looking dumb.

After a while, the little old lady began to respond. She pulled her door open a bit wider, allowing us to see how incredibly small she was. She started to nod, and mumble. '*Si . . . si . . .*' she said. '*Si, capisco . . .*' She was wearing a black dress, and her thin, silvery hair was pulled back in a bun. Most of her teeth seemed to be missing. '*Li conosco,*' she said. (I think.) '*Molto triste . . . povera femmina. Povera bambina.*'

Finally she began to gabble away excitedly, plucking at Peter's sleeve, waving her hand in the direction of Bettina's house. I saw Peter's expression become intent. He asked a couple of questions ('*Quando?*' '*Perché?*'), and listened to her reply at great length and in great detail. She kept clicking her tongue and shaking her head; I got the impression that something really shameful had happened next door.

'What does she say?' I murmured; but Peter flapped a hand at me. I sighed, and waited. Finally, Mrs Fanciulli began to run out of steam. She had to catch her breath, giving Peter a chance to interrupt. He thanked her several times. She responded with another burst of Italian, but it was a short one. He flushed, and stammered: '*Vicenza.*'

'*Ah! Vicenza!*' she exclaimed, while he backed down the stairs. '*Sono Napolana. Napoli hai visitato?*'

Peter shook his head. 'No,' he mumbled, and thanked her again.

'*Prego,*' she said.

'*Arrivederci,*' he replied.

He marched back up the path so briskly that I only drew level with him when he reached the street.

'Well?' I questioned. 'What was that all about?'

He stopped, and took a deep breath.

'Well,' he said, glancing at the Fanciulli house. '*That* was interesting.'

'Why?' gasped Bettina, hurrying to catch up. 'What did she tell you?'

'Plenty,' Peter rejoined. He looked a bit red and ruffled. 'That lady knew the people who used to live in your house two years ago,' he informed Bettina, speaking quietly. 'There were two sisters, called Alice and Terri Amirault, and Alice's boyfriend, and Terri's baby. The baby's name was Eloise.'

He paused for a moment. I said: 'Go on. Was there a dog or a cat?'

For some reason, Peter fixed me with a funny look. I was about to ask him what the matter was when he revealed that the baby, Eloise, had died.

In the house.

Alone.

'The mother was a drug addict,' Peter murmured. 'She went out and left the baby locked in the house. When she finally came back, it was dead.'

Bettina covered her mouth with her hand.

I didn't know what to say.

'According to Mrs Fanciulli,' Peter concluded, his fists wedged deep in his pockets, 'the baby died of starvation.'

CHAPTER # eight

I was horrified when I heard about Eloise. It honestly made me sick to my stomach. The thought of a little baby, crying and crying, its cries becoming weaker and weaker . . . well, it was dreadful. Just dreadful.

Bettina obviously felt the same. She went red, and her eyes filled with tears. Even Peter looked shaken.

'Horrible, eh?' he said. 'Spooky.'

'It must have happened in Bettina's bedroom,' I quavered. 'What are we going to do?'

'I'm never going in there again!' Bettina yelped. 'Never ever!'

'We'll have to tell your mum,' Peter pointed out. So we did. We went straight back to Bettina's house and told her mum, who went white when she heard.

'Who said this?' she demanded. 'That old woman next door? She's crazy.'

'No, Mum.' Bettina was pleading. 'She's Italian. Peter spoke to her. She knew the names and everything.'

'It would make sense,' Peter added grimly. 'A primitive hunger. You can't get much more primitive than a baby, can you?'

'It's nonsense,' Bettina's mum insisted, though she was still pale. 'You'll see. Tomorrow I'll call Community Housing. They'll tell me the truth.'

'I'm not sleeping in there, Mum.'

'Nobody asked you to!' Mrs Berich snapped. 'I told you, *I* will sleep there. I will sleep there and see what all the fuss is about.'

'Do you really think you should, Mrs Berich?' I couldn't help wondering if that was a good idea. 'Do you think anyone should?'

Mrs Berich muttered something in Croatian. Peter said: 'Maybe if you put some milk, or some baby food . . .'

'Oh, yes!' Bettina exclaimed. 'Maybe that would feed it!'

'Will you children *stop*?' Mrs Berich, who was wiping down the kitchen cupboards, suddenly threw her damp sponge into the sink. She put her hand to her forehead. 'Stop talking like this. Go and play.'

'Mum —'

'*Go and play.*'

Seeing that she was upset about something, we all tiptoed out of the kitchen. Then, without exchanging a single word, we went to stand at the door of Bettina's bedroom.

I couldn't have crossed the threshold. I couldn't have set foot in that room – not since learning what had happened in there. And yet it still looked quite ordinary. The green bedspread was slightly disturbed. The blinds were raised. A dusty cobweb trembled over the window.

Something about it made me feel sick all over again.

'It's like there's a coffin sitting in there,' Peter said at last, in hushed tones. 'I don't even want to go in.'

'Me neither,' Bettina whispered.

I turned away. All at once I was desperate for some fresh air. When Peter caught up with me, on the front doorstep, he asked me what was wrong.

'You look green,' he remarked.

'This is worse than Eglantine.' I blurted it out as if the words themselves tasted bad. 'I don't know why. I never felt sick with Eglantine. Not like this.'

'Because Eglantine died a long time ago,' Peter reminded me. 'Eloise has only been dead two years.'

'Maybe it's the same carpet,' choked Bettina, who had joined us. 'Maybe it's the same venetian blinds, and the same paint.'

We all stared at each other. Peter winced.

'God,' he said hoarsely. 'I never thought of that.'

'I have to call Mum.' It sounded rude, the way I said it, but I couldn't help myself. 'I'm going somewhere for dinner. I have to get home. Do you want a lift?'

'You should phone Delora again,' Peter suggested, ignoring the question. 'She might know what to do.'

'She won't know what to do.'

'Why not?'

'You heard what she said. She said she wouldn't connect. She said a force like that could cause a lot of damage. Do you want a *lift*, Peter?'

'But if you told her that it was a baby –'

'We don't know that it's a baby. We won't know until Mrs Berich talks to those housing people.'

'Well, okay,' Peter conceded. 'But if we find out there *was* an Eloise, and she *did* die in there –'

'I'm phoning my mum,' I interrupted, and turned to go inside. Peter grabbed my arm.

'Allie,' he said, 'what's the matter?'

He wasn't cross, just puzzled. Maybe a bit concerned. It was awful, because I didn't *want* to be gruff like that. If I hadn't been on the edge of tears, I would have been nicer.

'Sorry,' I sniffed, wiping my nose. 'I can't do this.'

Peter waited.

'This is too much for me,' I continued, trying not to cry. Everything was all muddled in my head, and knotted up in my stomach, but I knew that I wanted to get away from that room. 'I can't help with this, it's too . . .' (Real? Recent?) 'It's too horrible.'

'But you've *got* to help!' Bettina protested shrilly. 'We've got to do something!'

'It's true, Allie,' said Peter. He was still holding my arm. 'What about poor Bettina?'

'I know, but –'

'What about the poor baby?'

'Don't!' I jerked away, because I didn't want to think about the baby. Peter narrowed his eyes at me.

'What is it?' he asked. 'Are you – did you feel something? Or see something?'

'No. I don't know. I felt sick.' But I understood that Peter was right. Something had to be done – for Bettina *and* the baby. The poor, dead baby. 'I'll ring Delora,' I promised. 'See if she can help.'

'And you should leave some milk in that room overnight,' Peter instructed Bettina, who said: 'You mean cow's milk or that other stuff? That special baby's milk?'

'What special baby's milk?' I didn't know what she was talking about. To my surprise, however, Peter did.

'Formula,' he mumbled. 'It's called formula.'

'Is it expensive?' Bettina wanted to know, and I felt sorry for her.

'We'll pay you back out of the club funds,' I promised. 'In fact, I'll pay your share of Delora's fee, to make up for the formula. But you other guys,' I added, glancing at Peter, 'should pay *me* back as soon as you can. Like at school tomorrow, or something.'

'You should tell Michelle, then,' he observed.

'I will. I'll call her tonight, and remind her about the ten dollars. I'll tell her . . . I'll tell her what we found out, too.'

I must have gone green again, or at least looked sick, because Peter asked me gently if I wanted *him* to inform Michelle. It was really nice of him. I said that it might be better if he did it, because I was going out for dinner.

'Where are you going?' Bettina asked – almost wistfully, I thought. Perhaps she doesn't eat out much.

'Oh . . . nowhere,' I mumbled. The last thing I wanted to do was start talking about Dad. I had a funny sort of feeling that if I even *mentioned* moving in with him, then it might actually happen. I know things don't necessarily go away if you ignore them, but that's how I felt. 'Okay. So I'll call Delora, and Peter will call Michelle.'

'And I'll make sure that Mum calls Community Housing,' Bettina broke in. 'Tomorrow.'

'Right.'

'And we'll take it from there,' said Peter, with a sidelong glance at me. Then he finally informed me that he would like a lift, thank you very much, and I passed that information on to Mum when I spoke to her on the phone. We didn't talk much afterwards. Peter just kept looking at me in a funny way on the trip back to his place; I don't know if he was afraid that I was having a nervous breakdown, or fascinated by the thought that I'd somehow been affected by the force in Bettina's bedroom. Both, perhaps. It seemed odd that he hadn't been more affected himself.

Or maybe it wasn't terribly odd. When I saw Michelle the next day, she was excited rather than upset, so maybe there *is* something special about me. That 'dark aura', or whatever it is. Maybe I respond more to paranormal vibrations than other people do – unless I've just got a better imagination. It's possible that Michelle never pictured that little baby, crying and crying . . .

Or was I just on edge anyway, because of Dad?

Whatever the reason, I'm getting ahead of myself. Before I talk about Monday, I should describe Sunday night – the dinner at Dad's house, in other words. Dad lived in a really small terrace house in Newtown. It was right on the street, and you walked straight through the front door into the living room. Then there was a narrow hall leading down to the kitchen, past two bedrooms, and the bathroom was off the kitchen to the left. I thought to myself: this is *way* too small for Bethan and me. We couldn't possibly live here. And I was relieved, until it occurred to me that my dad could always move. To somewhere more spacious.

I was afraid to ask if he was going to. Just in case he said 'yes'.

Everything was very dark, because there were hardly any windows. Also, most of the overhead lights were turned off. Instead there were candles everywhere, and a few lamps with pink and green shawls draped over them. Everywhere you looked there were shadow puppets hanging on the walls and gold-embroidered cushions on the floor and incense sticks poking out of bits of Chinese pottery. The whole place smelled of incense, or something like that. Bethan asked if he could open a window.

'You don't like my aromatic oils?' asked Matoaka, who wasn't what I had expected. I suppose I thought she'd be Asian, or something, but she wasn't. Her name was Matoaka Purkis. She had blue eyes and brown hair and looked a bit like Mrs Procter, our library teacher, only fatter. She was wearing a batik sarong around her waist, as a skirt, and an Indian cotton top that jingled. Her nose was sunburned.

'They're very nice oils,' I said, coughing, 'only Bethan's allergic to patchouli. His nose swells up.'

Matoaka frowned.

'I don't know if there's patchouli in the jasmine oil,' she began.

But Bethan was firm. 'I can't breathe,' he declared.

So Matoaka had to go around blowing out all her scented candles and things. Dad, who was dressed in a sarong, too, showed us how we'd be sitting on the polished wooden floor and eating out of bowls, with our fingers. Bethan liked that. He also liked the ferocious wooden mask in the bathroom. (Matoaka said it was there to scare away cockroaches.) He didn't like the wine, though, and he made Dad get him some Pepsi. I was really, *really* surprised that they had it in the house. Matoaka explained that it belonged to one of the other people who lived there.

'So how was the séance?' she said, changing the

104

subject as we all seized our first handfuls of rice and passed the bowl around. 'Jim told me you held a séance, last night.'

'Uh, yeah.' I felt embarrassed, because my séance was the reason we hadn't been able to accept her first invitation. 'Yeah, it was okay.'

'What happened?'

'Nothing much.' Actually, I don't like eating food with my fingers, because I tend to drop rice everywhere. Also, the coconut curry was making my hangnail sting. 'Sorry about the mess,' I said.

'Oh, don't worry. That's why we're sitting on the floor,' Matoaka tinkled.

'It's one reason, anyway,' my father added. 'The other reason is that we don't have a proper table.'

'Why not?' asked Bethan. (He doesn't like curry, but was doing his best with the rice, melon and yoghurt.)

'No room.' Dad was looking at me, licking his fingers. 'Did your mother attend this séance?'

'Yeah.'

'And may I ask what purpose it served?'

I didn't know how to answer that, especially since Dad's tone was a bit sarcastic. Fortunately, however, Matoaka butted in.

'Yes, what were you trying to do?' she inquired, sounding genuinely interested. Unlike Dad, who was obviously used to sitting cross-legged, she kept shifting and wriggling and changing her position. 'Were you trying to reach somebody specific?'

'Yeah.'

'But you didn't,' Dad said flatly.

'No.' I really didn't want to talk about it. Bethan, however, looked up from the rice that he was picking off his leg and remarked: 'I thought you told Ray that the house was haunted?'

'No, I didn't.'

'Yes, you did. I heard you. Last night, when you came home.'

'I said it *might* be haunted.'

'And then you said you were going back there today, to ask the neighbours.' Yoghurt was dribbling down Bethan's arm. 'Dad, can I have a spoon, please?'

'Yes, perhaps you'd better.' Dad got up to fetch a spoon. Matoaka leaned towards me. One of her teeth was grey, and she had a red nose stud so small that from a distance it looked like a little pimple.

'What makes you think the house is haunted?' she queried, smiling an encouraging smile. 'Have you any idea who might be haunting it?'

'Uh, well . . .'

'I thought you said it was a dog,' big-mouth Bethan remarked. This time he was picking bits of rice off the floor and putting them in his mouth.

'It's not a dog,' I retorted crossly. 'Bethan, don't do that, it's disgusting!'

'You said it was a dog,' he insisted.

'I said it *might* be a dog. But it isn't.'

'How do you know?'

'Because . . .' I hesitated, as Dad returned with a spoon. He gave it to Bethan, and sat down again. 'Because it's probably a baby,' I sighed.

'A *baby*?'

'We think a baby died in the house,' I mumbled. 'One of the neighbours said so.'

'Now you see, that's what I'm talking about,' Dad frowned. He was shaking his head. 'That's the sort of nasty thing you're going to get messed up in, holding séances. I warned your mother. I told her. It's not enriching, it's a drain. It's spiritually draining.'

'It can throw your balance out of whack,' Matoaka agreed, through a mouthful of curry. 'But that's easily sorted. I can align her tonight, Jim, if that's what you're worried about.'

Align me?

'Uh, no thanks,' I said quickly. 'I'm fine.'

'Are you sure?' Matoaka peered into my face. 'Your colour's not too good.'

'That's probably her diet,' said Dad. 'It's pretty toxic, from what I can see.'

Toxic! Before I could protest, however, Bethan observed in absent-minded tones: 'She looks green because of that stuff on the lamp. We all look green, except you, Dad.' He was trying to spread yoghurt on a slice of melon with the edge of his spoon. 'You look kind of purple.'

'Well, be that as it may,' said Dad, 'I don't think you should be involved in this business, Alethea. It can't be good for you.'

I had a funny sort of feeling that he was right. So why was I annoyed? 'Someone has to do something,' I replied stiffly. 'My friend won't be able to sleep in her own bedroom, otherwise.'

'Oh, that's not a problem,' Matoaka exclaimed. 'You just want to cleanse it. A Sioux purifying ceremony, that's what you want. Does the trick every time.'

'A what?' I had to ask.

'Sioux,' she repeated. 'A Sioux purifying ceremony. Don't you know the Sioux? They're one of the First Nations.' I stared at her blankly, and she went on. 'Native North Americans? You know?'

'She means Red Indians,' Bethan supplied, and drew a frown from our father.

'We don't use that term, Bethan,' he reproved gently. 'It's insulting.'

'I've been to a whole bunch of ceremonies in South Dakota, when I was on the reservation, and I've seen some amazing things,' Matoaka revealed, wiping her mouth and scrambling to her feet. 'Anyone for naan bread? I forgot the naan bread.'

'Are you In – I mean, are *you* Native American?' I had been struck by a sudden thought: perhaps Matoaka was her real name after all? She took a deep breath, and placed a hand on her chest, looking off into the distance.

'In my heart, I am,' she replied. 'In my heart, I'm of the Powhatan. There's a connection, I know that.'

'The way you've responded to it, Mat, there must be,' my father concurred. I got the feeling that they'd

108

discussed the matter before. 'Mat had a really deep, visceral response to the Powhatan culture,' he explained to me. 'She underwent a shamanic ritual, and she was transfigured. She really did reach the next level.'

'I saw my spirit guide,' Matoaka beamed. 'I've been told that I'm a reincarnation of Matoaka. That's why I changed my name.'

'Matoaka?' I was completely lost.

'Pocahontas,' Dad translated. 'Matoaka was her real name. Her Powhatan name.'

'Oh.'

'That was a dumb movie,' Bethan suddenly observed. 'It was boring.'

'Somehow I don't think Disney captured the essence of the Powhatan experience,' Dad said drily, and Matoaka continued, as if she hadn't heard: 'The Playful One forged connections between two cultures, which is my role as well. It's a destiny that transcends Time.'

I don't know what she was talking about, exactly, but at least it wasn't Eloise. From then on we discussed reincarnation, and Ancient Egypt, and the constellation of Orion, and what Bethan and I normally ate at school.

All the while, an unasked question was pounding in my head – a question that I never had the guts to ask.

Would we, or would we not, be invited to live with our father?

CHAPTER # nine

I met Michelle at our bus stop the next morning, and we talked about Eloise. Michelle was very excited. She kept wondering aloud why no one had heard the baby, whether anyone had been arrested and put in gaol, whether it was the mother who had found Eloise after she died – that kind of thing. The kind of thing I didn't want to think about. Then the bus arrived, with Bettina already on it, and we learned something new.

'Mum let me put a cup of formula in the room, last night,' Bettina informed us, 'but she drank it all herself. She couldn't help it.'

'Your *mum* drank the formula?' I exclaimed.

'Every last drop. As well as a whole packet of rice crackers, and all the cheese, and –'

'She slept in your room, then?' Michelle wanted to know.

'Oh, yes. And I slept in hers.' Bettina's forehead was creased. She looked tired and worried. 'My mother didn't sleep well. Auntie Astra didn't sleep well – she cries a lot . . .'

I felt instantly guilty.

'. . . and I didn't sleep well either,' Bettina confessed. 'I was worried about Mum, in that room.'

'Is she going to call Community Housing?' asked Michelle.

'Oh, yes. As soon as she can.' Bettina chewed at her bottom lip. 'She's very upset.'

I wasn't surprised. I was pretty upset myself. For the first time, I wondered if Matoaka's Sioux purifying ceremony might do some good, but then I remembered my mother's Chinese Feng Shui purifying ceremony.

Feng Shui hadn't got rid of Eglantine. Why would a Native American ritual get rid of Eloise? Eloise hadn't been Native American, as far as we knew.

'Maybe we should get a bottle,' I remarked, as the bus chugged to a halt at Peter's stop. I could see him surging through the door. Heading down the aisle.

Michelle and Bettina stared at me.

'What?' said Michelle.

'Maybe we should get a bottle,' I repeated. 'A baby's bottle. Maybe the formula didn't work because it was in a cup.'

'Or maybe Eloise just doesn't like formula,' Peter suggested, throwing himself into the seat behind me. 'Some babies don't.'

'How would *you* know?' Michelle said sceptically, and Peter shrugged.

'My nephew wouldn't drink formula,' he explained. 'Not until he was nearly one. Only, you know . . .' He went a bit red. 'Breast milk.'

'You have a nephew?' I couldn't believe it. 'You mean you're an uncle? *You?*'

'Yeah.' He sounded defensive. 'What's wrong with that?'

'You're too young!' Michelle exclaimed.

'My oldest sister is nineteen. She's married. She has a baby.' Peter was obviously put out. 'What's so strange about that?'

'Nothing,' I said hastily. It did seem strange that Peter had never mentioned his nephew before, but then again, maybe it wasn't so strange. Boys aren't much interested in babies. And you don't always tell your friends everything.

I hadn't told my friends about Dad, for instance. I knew I would have to, very soon. I just didn't want to be answering certain questions, like: Are you going to move in with him?

'My nephew wouldn't touch formula until he was eleven months old,' Peter was saying. 'Maybe Eloise wouldn't either.'

'Or maybe she won't drink from a cup,' Michelle

declared. 'Like Allie said. How old do babies have to be, to drink from cups?'

She was asking me, for some reason. I shrugged.

'I don't know,' I said.

'Neither do I,' Bettina added.

We three girls turned to Peter, who went red again.

'It's no good looking at me!' he protested. 'How should I know?'

'Well, does your nephew drink from a cup?' I inquired.

'No. Just a bottle, now. But other babies might be different.'

'If only we knew how old Eloise was,' Michelle sighed, and I nodded.

'The trouble is that we don't know enough about her at all,' I said. 'All we have is gossip from Mrs Fanciulli. We don't even know if she really existed.'

'My mum will find all that out,' Bettina assured us.

She did, too – and she passed it on – but not until later. Not until after school. Bettina called my house when my whole family was sitting in the kitchen, eating lamb cutlets – and since we have a rule in our house about how phone calls during dinner have to be kept short, I wasn't able to discuss all the details with her. She did have time to tell me that Eloise Amirault had been three months old when she'd died, and that it had happened in Bettina's house. Twenty-two months previously.

'They didn't want Mum to know anything about it,' Bettina revealed. 'I don't think they would have told her, if Mum hadn't got so mad at them. Now she wants them to move us to another house, but of course she can't say why. They'd think she was crazy.'

'I know,' I said, remembering my experience with Eglantine.

'They wouldn't tell her anything else,' Bettina continued. 'Like what happened to the mother or who found the baby or anything.'

'Okay. Thanks, Bettina.'

'The mother *was* a heroin addict, by the way. Mum found *that* out.'

'Oh.'

'Awful, isn't it?'

It was. When I returned to the dinner table, I didn't feel hungry. Mum said: 'Who was that?'

'Bettina.'

'What's wrong?' asked Ray, and I saw that he was looking at me the way he does sometimes, calmly but intently.

'Oh . . .' I began to push my mashed potato around. 'She found out something.'

'About the ghost?' Bethan mumbled, through a mouthful of food. 'Is it a baby or a dog?'

'A what?' Mum exclaimed, and I sighed.

'It's a baby,' I admitted. 'Mrs Berich found out that a three-month-old baby called Eloise Amirault died of starvation in Bettina's house. Nearly two years ago.'

Mum winced. Bethan kept shovelling food down his throat. Ray said quietly: 'That's not good.'

'No. It's awful.' I rearranged the vegetables on my plate. 'Its mother was a heroin addict,' I added.

Mum frowned. She wiped her lips with her napkin. 'This is the same room that Delora had trouble with, I take it,' she said.

'Yeah. The one that makes everyone hungry.'

'Oh, right.' Ray began to nod. 'I recall, now – you mentioned it.'

'Yes. And no one wants to sleep in that bedroom any more. And Mrs Berich wants to move.'

Gazing around the table, I realised what a relief it was to discuss a ghost with grown-ups who didn't laugh or sneer or get cross. Suddenly I felt as if I could talk about Eloise, at long last. The words just came tumbling out.

'Bettina's mum and sister have both slept in her bedroom, and ended up eating everything in sight,' I explained. 'They tried leaving food in there, too – last night they left a cup of baby's formula – but it didn't work. Mrs Berich drank the formula.'

Mum made a face. 'That stuff?' she said. 'Yuk.'

'I was thinking that maybe Eloise wasn't satisfied because the formula was in a cup instead of a bottle,' I went on, 'but Peter thinks maybe she doesn't like formula. "Some babies don't," he says.'

'So you think you have to find out what this baby wants?' Ray said. 'And if you do, and you give it to her, then she'll go away?'

'Like Eglantine,' I agreed. 'This baby's hungry, so we figured she must want food.'

'Why don't they just make that bedroom a dining room?' Bethan demanded. 'Then it won't matter if people feel hungry in there.'

'It's more complicated than that,' I replied, trying to be patient with him. 'Bettina's family aren't just worried about being hungry in there. They hate the *ghost* being in there. You would, too. You know what it was like with Eglantine.'

'Can't Delora do something?' Ray was slowly cutting up his eggplant (which Mum hadn't bothered giving to Bethan and me: we hate eggplant). 'Surely Delora would be able to help? She helped with Eglantine.'

'I dunno,' I mumbled. 'Maybe.' I was thinking about the money that Delora might charge, and the tone of her voice when she'd said, 'A force like that could cause a lot of damage.'

And then Mum spoke. She put down her glass of wine, folded her napkin beside her plate, and said quietly, 'Well, it's perfectly obvious, isn't it?'

We all stared at her.

'There's one thing that all babies want. All the time,' she announced, her gaze moving from face to face. 'They want their mothers.'

I blinked. Bethan chewed. Ray nodded again.

'Yes, of course,' he said.

'But – but –' I couldn't believe that Mum was serious. 'But the mother *killed* Eloise. She left her in the house, all alone.'

'The baby wouldn't know that,' Mum said. 'How old

116

did you say she was? Three months? A baby that age wouldn't know anything. Just that she wanted her mother.'

I swallowed.

Mum's eyes, I could see, were suddenly full of tears. I suppose it *was* sad, that a baby should have wanted the mother who neglected her.

In fact, it was so sad that I didn't really want to think about it.

'The trouble is, we don't know where to find the mother,' I pointed out, after a long pause. 'She could be in gaol. She could be anywhere.'

'You could look in the phone book,' Ray suggested.

'Or on the internet,' said Bethan.

'Or you could check the local rag,' Ray continued. He sat with his fork poised over his meat. 'Local newspapers always run items on things like that.'

'But it was two years ago,' I objected.

'So? They'll have back issues at the library.'

'Really?'

'Bound to. Or you can try the newspaper office. Someone will have kept copies.'

'I'll take you tomorrow,' Mum offered. 'I'll pick you up from school, and I'll take you to the library, and you can check.'

'Oh.' I was astonished – and pleased. 'Thanks, Mum.'

'There's nothing worse,' she concluded, 'than a troubled spirit in a family bedroom.'

I reported all this to the Exorcists' Club the next

117

morning. Michelle was envious; she wished aloud that *her* mum was as helpful as mine, when it came to ghosts. Bettina was relieved; she and Mrs Berich had spent the previous night in the same double bed, and Bettina wasn't used to sharing.

Peter nodded thoughtfully.

'So we're going to search for the mother, is that it?' he asked me.

'I guess.'

'And then what? I mean, suppose she's in gaol?'

It was a good question. I looked helplessly at Michelle, who shrugged.

'Maybe Delora will have an idea,' she said.

'Maybe.' Suddenly I remembered Delora's forty-dollar fee. 'You still owe me ten dollars, by the way. Both of you.'

'Oh, yeah.' Michelle fished around in her bag. Peter dug into his pocket. We had just got off the bus, and were standing in front of the school gates.

'The formula only cost five dollars,' Bettina said awkwardly, as I collected everyone's share. 'But if you want me to buy a baby's bottle, too . . .'

'Buy the bottle,' I decided. 'You might as well.'

'Not if I can borrow one from my sister,' Peter offered. 'She has plenty. She wouldn't mind. I'll ask her, the next time she comes to our place.'

'When will that be?' Michelle inquired.

'Oh, I dunno. This weekend?'

There was a pause. Then Bettina said, in a small

voice, 'It would be better if we didn't have to wait until the weekend.'

So it was decided that Bettina would buy a baby's bottle and try it out in her bedroom. If that didn't work, she could give the bottle to Peter, who would give it to his sister, who might even give Bettina her money back. By the time the bell went, it had all been settled.

What's more, at lunchtime I sorted something else out. I was on duty in the school library, and it occurred to me that Mrs Procter might know if the public library kept back copies of the local newspaper. When I asked her, she looked at me with her head cocked to one side, like a bird, and said: 'What makes you think you have to go to the public library?'

I didn't understand, at first. 'What do you mean?'

'I mean that I keep my own copies,' she answered, with a little smile.

'You do?'

'Since I came here. For school projects. Local history projects, and that kind of thing.'

'Where are they?'

Mrs Procter clicked her tongue, but she was still smiling. 'You should know, Allie,' she scolded. 'You're supposed to be my best library monitor.'

'Reference section?' I hazarded.

'Let's have a look.'

They *were* in the Reference section – four big red books, each containing fifty-two bound copies of the local newspaper. I looked for the volume covering the month when Eloise died, and Mrs Procter helped me carry it to a reading table. By this time, Michelle and Bettina were both hovering around, excitedly.

'Okay,' I said, leafing through the crackling pages. 'Twenty-two months ago. That would be October . . .'

'Here!' Michelle exclaimed.

'Okay. You take the left side, and I'll take the right side.'

'What about me?' Bettina piped up.

'You keep an eye on Scott McLoughlin,' Michelle ordered. 'He's going to start making trouble, I just know it.'

From over near her desk, Mrs Procter suddenly asked us what we were looking for. It was an awkward moment. When I finally told her that we wanted to find out about someone who'd died, she advised us to check the obituaries. Down near the back of the paper.

Of course, we weren't looking for the obituaries. We were looking for a news story, like the one that this same newspaper had run about Eglantine. My eyes ran down the columns of print, past *Council Loses Court Case*, *Arrests in Warehouse*, *Local Ballerina Hits Big Time*. We turned the page. *Development Gets Green Light*, *Health Department Raid*, *Local Business Owner Up in Arms*. There were five newspapers to read, and we had to do it as quickly as possible, not bothering with more than the headlines and first paragraphs.

We didn't find what we were looking for until we reached the third newspaper.

120

'There!' Michelle cried. 'Look!'

I looked. *Baby Dies in Tragic Circumstances*, I read. *A twenty-two-year-old woman has been arrested after the death of her three-month-old daughter in what a DOCS representative has described as 'tragic circumstances'* . . .

'This is it,' I croaked, and started to read aloud. '. . . *The child's body was discovered by two other occupants of the house when they returned from an interstate trip.* It doesn't give any names, or anything, but the mother was arrested.'

'The question is, did she go to gaol?' Michelle remarked.

'I don't know. It doesn't say.'

'Maybe in the next edition. Maybe there was a trial, or something.'

'Let's just photocopy this article, first.'

We split the cost of a photocopy, and then continued to flip through the volume of newspapers. We tried the next issue, and the one after that, and the one after that. We scanned three months' worth of newspapers before the bell went – without finding a thing. It was very frustrating. We had to tear ourselves away, even though we were desperate to know whether Terri Amirault had gone to gaol or not.

When we told Peter at the bus stop that afternoon, he offered us an explanation.

'These things can take months and months to come to trial,' he said 'Either you missed the story, or you never even got to it.'

'Or it's not even there,' I added gloomily. 'Maybe they never followed up.'

'How do you know so much about trials?' Michelle asked Peter, who shrugged.

'I just do. From my mum's work.'

'She's not a lawyer, is she? I thought you said she was a nurse, or something?'

'A lot of her clients are loonies,' said Peter. 'A lot of them end up in court.' He adjusted his backpack, 'Why don't we call the journalist?' he asked, with a nod at our photocopy. 'Why don't we call Ned Sandstrom?'

'The man who wrote it?' I frowned. 'Do you think he's still working there?'

'Why not? It was only two years ago. And he'll know the inside story.'

'But will he talk to us?'

'He will if we tell him about the ghost,' said Michelle.

I glanced at Peter, who glanced at Bettina, who glanced back at me. For a while, no one said anything. Around us, kids shrieked and chattered and punched each other. Bethan, I noticed, was staggering around with somebody's schoolbag pulled down over his head.

'I don't think we should tell Ned Sandstrom about the ghost,' I volunteered at last.

'Neither do I,' Bettina chimed in. She looked scared. 'My mum would kill me.' All at once her eyes widened, and she put her hand over her mouth. 'I mean – I don't mean –'

'We know what you mean,' said Peter.

Michelle seemed to be pondering.

'If we don't tell him about the ghost, what are we going to tell him?' She leaned towards the rest of us, lowering her voice. 'We have to have a reason for being interested in Eloise.'

'Bettina has a reason,' Peter pointed out. 'She lives in the same house.'

'Oh, but I couldn't – I mean, I don't want to –'

'It's all right, Bettina.' I patted her arm. 'I'll call him, and I'll say I'm you.'

At that moment Mum arrived, all dressed up in her bank clothes. As I helped her to round up Bethan (who had discarded the schoolbag, and was doing stupid things with somebody's striped sock), I told her that I wouldn't have to go to the library after all. I'd already found what I wanted.

'Mrs Procter helped me,' I explained. 'I got a photo-copy of the article.'

'Well done,' said Mum.

'And I'm going to phone the man who wrote it. Mum? Where are you going?'

'Back to the bus line, of course,' she replied. 'Won't Michelle want a lift, too?'

She did. So did Peter. But I knew that if Mum saw Bettina unlocking her own front door, she might realise that I had been on an 'unsupervised visit' the first time I went there, and would demand an explanation.

That's why, when the question arose as to whether four kids could somehow squeeze into the back of our car, I pulled a face at Bettina, who assured Mum that she didn't need a lift.

'It's all right, Mrs Gebhardt,' she said, watching me out of the corner of her eye as I mimed a seatbelt. 'Er . . . it would be against the law.'

'Against the law?'

'Not enough seatbelts.'

'Oh, but it's not far.'

'No, thank you. Anyway, my mum doesn't like me getting lifts unless I ask first.'

'Not even with me?'

I shook my head. Bettina shook her head. At which point Mum gave up (thank goodness) and shepherded everyone – except poor Bettina – back to our car.

I felt bad when I peered over my shoulder, and saw Bettina standing there all alone. Even though I smiled, and gave her a thumbs-up sign, and mouthed the word 'sorry', I still felt bad. I thought to myself: I'll call her later. And explain.

I don't know if Michelle and Peter shared my guilt. They started talking about Eloise the minute they'd fastened their seatbelts.

'If we can find out where the mother went,' Michelle announced, 'and she's not in gaol, then maybe we can get her to come back to the house. Maybe if she actually appears, then Eloise will be satisfied.'

'I don't know,' Peter objected. 'What happens when

124

the mother goes away again? We'll be back to square one, won't we? Unless there's some way she can take the baby along.'

'Like in a *box*?' said Michelle, sarcastically.

'No.' Peter shot her a withering glance. 'I mean there might be a way of getting a spirit to attach itself to something. Like a genie in a bottle. I bet Delora would know.'

'Delora won't touch this ghost,' I reminded him. 'You know that, Peter. She's scared of it.'

'Well, what are we going to do, then?' said Peter. 'I mean, Bettina can't exactly ask the mother to move in with them permanently, can she?'

Then Mum cleared her throat, in a way that I've come to recognise. It always means that she has something to say.

'Kids,' she said, as she pulled up in front of Peter's house, 'I want you to think for a moment.' She turned in her seat to face us, while Bethan munched on half a packet of stale Twisties beside her. 'If you were a woman whose addiction had resulted in the death of your only child, and you were told that your child was now a ghost, haunting someone's house, how do you think you'd feel?'

I scratched my neck. Peter scratched his knee. Michelle said hopefully, 'Pleased? I mean, at least I'd be able to see my kid again. Like Astra wants to.'

'Wrong,' Mum replied. 'It would be so traumatic, so unimaginably awful, that I'd want nothing to do with the people who told me about it. *Nothing.*'

I was almost frightened by the tone of Mum's voice. It was so serious. So firm and harsh.

Peter swallowed, audibly.

'Well, maybe we should just take it one step at a time,' he mumbled, and climbed out of the car.

We were all pretty quiet for the rest of the trip.

CHAPTER # ten

I rang Bettina as soon as I arrived home to explain why I'd left her in the bus line. (She was very understanding.) Then I rang the local paper and asked for Ned Sandstrom. He wasn't in. So I left a message, and went to finish my history project.

When the phone jangled about an hour later, I rushed downstairs again to grab it, thinking that Ned Sandstrom might be returning my call. But I recognised the voice at the other end of the line. It was my father's.

'Alethea? Is that you?'

'Oh. Hi, Dad.'

'You don't sound very happy to hear from me.'

'Oh, I am. Really. I was just – I was just doing my homework.'

'Well, I'm sorry to interrupt. I wanted to ask if you'd like to come out with me tomorrow night. Another dinner. Just you and me.'

'Oh!' I glanced at Bethan, who was riding his scooter down the hallway. 'Well, that would be great, but –'

'I'll take Bethan out another night. Friday, maybe. One on one. I think that might be a good idea, don't you?'

'I guess.' Worried that Ned Sandstrom might be trying to call, I was eager to get off the phone. 'Sure. Tomorrow night. What time?'

'Not too late, obviously. Say, six o'clock?'

'Okay. Great. Bye, Dad.'

'Wait! Hang on. Hadn't you better ask your mother?'

'Oh. Right. Sure. I'll do that.' (But where was she? Out in the garden?) 'Uh, what if I call you back if there's a problem?'

'Yes, all right. That should work.'

'Bye, then. Bye.'

I broke the connection as Bethan whizzed past. 'Where's Mum?' I called after him.

'Dunno.'

'Is she in the studio?'

'Dunno.'

He disappeared out the back door. I was about to follow him when the phone rang again, and this time it *was* Ned Sandstrom. He had a gravelly voice, and sounded quite old (not to mention tired and impatient). But when I mentioned his article about Eloise, he seemed to brighten up a bit.

'Oh, yeah,' he said. 'I remember that. What's your interest?'

'My friend lives in the same house, now,' I explained, with my heart in my throat. 'She wants to know what happened.'

'I see.' A sigh. 'Well, you saw the story, didn't you? Mother was off on a bender, sister came home with the boyfriend –'

'No, I mean, what happened to the mother? Did she go to gaol?'

'Oh!' There was a long pause. I could hear noises in the background: clattering, chattering noises. 'I'm trying to think,' he said at last. 'Yeah, I think I covered that, too. Yeah, I remember. Suspended sentence. They stuck her in a treatment centre. It was that one up the road from here, you know the one?'

'No,' I confessed.

'Oh, what's its name? Warriewood. Warriewood Drug Rehabilitation Centre. Lot of people go there instead of prison. Try to sort themselves out.' Suddenly his tone changed. 'How old are you, anyway?'

'Twelve.'

'Ah.'

'Thank you very much. My friend was interested.'

And I hung up, before he started to ask *me* questions. Then I stood for a while, thinking. Warriewood Drug Rehabilitation Centre. It was bound to be in the phone book. Should I call, I wondered, and ask about Terri Amirault? Would there be any point? A drug rehabilitation centre sounded like a scary place. It sounded like the sort of place where people might not want to talk to little kids – especially to little kids looking for information on past residents.

Hesitantly, I flicked through the second volume of our White Pages, and quickly found Warriewood Drug Rehabilitation Centre. There was only one number, printed in big, bold letters. I have to admit, I don't like ringing up total strangers. I get quite nervous. Ned Sandstrom had been bad enough, but Warriewood sounded much worse.

Then I thought about Peter and Michelle, and how disappointed they would be if I turned up at school, the next morning, without having at least tried to find out about Terri Amirault. They would wonder why I hadn't called. They might wonder if I had been scared.

Michelle wouldn't be scared, I knew. Michelle had no trouble asking shop assistants to get her things, or telling Year Five boys to be quiet.

I picked up the receiver, and punched in the eight-digit code. There were five rings followed by a woman's voice.

'Warriewood, how may I help you?' she said.

'Uh, hi.' I swallowed. 'My name's Allie Gebhardt, and I'm calling on behalf –'

'Allie *Gebhardt*?'

My jaw dropped.

'Would that be the same Allie Gebhardt who's a special friend of my son Peter?' the woman exclaimed.

'Uh –'

'It's Paula Cresciani, Allie. I'm Peter's mum.'

'Oh.'

'We met once, remember? At Peter's birthday party.'

'Oh, yeah.' I vaguely recalled Peter's mum, who had lots of grey hair and a big smile. 'Hi, Mrs Cresciani.'

'Peter's always talking about you. It's always "Allie, Allie, Allie".'

'Really?' I didn't know how to respond. 'Well, I like him, too.'

'He's a nice boy, my Peter. You should come over again, soon. Pay us a visit – we'd love that. *Peter* would love that.'

'Okay. Sure.' I was feeling embarrassed; I don't quite know why. 'That would be great.'

'Good! Any time! Now what's the matter, *cara*? Why are you calling this place?'

It was a relief to get to the point. Tugging at my socks, I stammered: 'Do you – do you work there, Mrs Cresciani?'

'I certainly do. Didn't Peter tell you?'

'Maybe.' Now that I thought about it, Peter *had* mentioned something about his mother being a nurse. 'You're a nurse, right?'

'A part-time psychiatric social worker.'

'Oh.'

'So what can I do for you, my love? Is everything all right?'

I asked if there was someone named Terri Amirault

131

currently living at Warriewood. No, Mrs Cresciani replied, there wasn't.

'Oh.' That was disappointing, though not entirely unexpected. It had been nearly two years, after all. 'Well, she was there once,' I continued. 'About two years ago. Do you know where she might have gone?'

'What's your interest, Allie?'

Oh, dear. I wasn't sure how much Peter's mum knew – or how much he wanted her to know. Suddenly I wished that I hadn't called.

'It's just – have you heard of Bettina Berich?' I said carefully.

'Bettina? Your little friend? Peter went over to her house, last week?'

'That's right.' At least she knew about Bettina. It was a start. 'Well . . . um . . . Terri used to live in Bettina's house. And Bettina wants to ask her something.'

'About the house?'

'Yes.'

'You mean it was trashed?'

'Uh, no, I – I don't think so. I don't know.' I had never really thought about *that*. 'Bettina just wants to ask about something that's been . . .' (That's been what?) '. . . that's been left behind.'

'I see.' A short silence. 'Well, you know, we don't normally give out information about our clients, Allie.'

'Oh.' What a blow. 'Not even if they don't live there any more?'

Instead of answering, Mrs Cresciani asked another question.

'What did she leave behind? Something she might need? Something important?'

'Well . . .' I didn't want to lie. 'She might not want it. I don't know.'

'So what is it, Allie?'

I was aware that if I said 'a ghost', I wouldn't have a chance of finding out where Terri had gone. Mrs Cresciani would probably think that I was playing some sort of stupid trick, or game.

'It's nothing,' I said. 'Don't worry.'

'You can tell me, *cara*, it's all right. I'll talk to the manager here, and see if we can help.'

'No, no. It's not important. Bye, Mrs Cresciani.'

I slammed down the receiver, my heart thudding. But of course I couldn't leave it at that. I had to ring Peter and warn him. I didn't want him unprepared for the moment when his mum came home, and interrogated him about my peculiar phone call.

He answered on the third ring, and seemed unconcerned when I explained what had happened. It would be all right, he said. He'd think of something.

'If we tell her it's a ghost, she won't lift a finger,' he conceded. 'We have to tell her something like . . . I dunno . . . like Bettina's family wants to perform a traditional purifying ceremony, and would like the mother's permission. She might go for that because it's a cultural thing, you see.'

'But . . .' I didn't know how to put this. 'But if you're lying, Peter, and she finds out –'

'Lying? Who said anything about lying?' Peter's voice sounded funny, as if he was munching on a sandwich. 'I mean, have we actually decided what we're going to do yet? Have we decided that we're *not* going to hold a purifying ceremony?'

'Well, no, but –'

'It's okay, Allie, I'll sort it out. And thanks for the warning.' After a moment's hesitation, he added: 'Did she say anything else?'

'About Terri? No.'

'About anything.'

'Like what?' I was stumped. 'What do you mean?'

'Nothing. It's nothing. She can be such an idiot, that's all.'

'Really?' She had seemed perfectly sensible to me. 'I thought she was nice. She asked me over to your place.'

Peter groaned. 'I knew it,' he spluttered.

'What?'

'Nothing. It doesn't matter. I'll see you tomorrow.'

He hung up. By this time it was getting late, and I had a history project to finish. So I rushed upstairs, thinking about Terri and Peter's mum and the Warriewood Drug Rehabilitation Centre, and what with one thing and another, I completely forgot about Dad's invitation.

It slipped my mind until the following evening. That's when I – well, when I stuffed up big time. But

I won't go into it yet. First of all I have to describe what happened the next day, because it was important. *Very* important.

As usual, I caught the bus in the morning. And as usual, I met Michelle at the bus stop, where I told her all about my phone calls of the night before. She listened eagerly, before offering to make the next bunch of calls, because she never got to do anything interesting – not like me and Peter. We disagreed about that. Then the bus arrived, and we found a seat down the back, near Bettina.

I'd never seen her looking so excited. Her cheeks were red, and her eyes were popping, and her hair seemed to be standing out all over her head. When we swung ourselves onto the seat in front of her, the words were already tumbling out of her mouth.

'Guess what, guess what, guess *what*?' she babbled. 'It worked! It worked, after all!'

'What?' I said.

'Huh?' said Michelle.

'The bottle! It worked!' She leaned forward. 'I put that bottle of formula in the room, last night, and it worked, Allie! It really worked!'

'You mean –'

'Auntie Astra slept in there last night, and she didn't drink it.'

'Yes, but –'

'She didn't eat anything, either! She wasn't hungry! So I went in there this morning, with my breakfast, and I *didn't finish my eggs!* I wasn't hungry at all, not one little bit!'

Michelle and I exchanged glances.

'That's great, Bettina,' I said.

'That's terrific,' Michelle agreed. We were both a bit stunned, I think. Personally, I had already given up on the bottle idea. It had seemed too easy.

'Auntie Astra wanted to talk to the baby ghost,' Bettina continued chattily. 'She said if Michael wasn't around, then perhaps the baby could tell her about him. She insisted on sleeping in my bedroom. And now she thinks the ghost was all a big lie, and she's argued with my mother, but I don't care, not now, because the ghost has *gone.*'

'Are you sure, though?' I couldn't quite believe it. 'How can you be sure?'

'I am sure.' Bettina nodded solemnly, just as our bus lurched to a halt at Peter's bus stop. 'One fresh bottle of formula every night, and that ghost won't bother me any more. I can feel it. In my bones.'

All the same, I was sceptical. Eglantine had been so hard to get rid of; was it really possible to exorcise a troubled spirit with one bottle of baby formula? Bettina said it was. Michelle didn't know. Peter, when asked, simply shrugged.

'Remember what Delora said,' he pointed out. 'Eloise is a lot more primitive than Eglantine. Perhaps that makes Eloise easier to satisfy.'

I grunted. For some reason I wasn't happy, though I

should have been, for Bettina's sake. Something was bugging me. As the others eagerly chattered about Eloise, and Astra, and Peter's mum (who hadn't promised to chase up Terri Amirault, despite Peter's attempts to persuade her), I stared out the window, chewing on my nails.

It was Peter who finally drew me aside, after we had got off the bus.

'Are you angry about something?' he queried, and I blinked at him in surprise.

'Who, me? No.'

'Then why aren't you talking to anyone?'

'I was just thinking.'

'About what?'

'About whether I should ask Delora to visit the Beriches' house, and see if she can still sense that ghost.'

Peter perked up a bit. We were standing near the assembly hall, and at that moment Tony Karavias stuck his big, ugly face between us and made smooching noises.

Peter swung at him, scowling.

'Piss off!'

'Cresciani's got the hots,' Tony cried, in a sing-song voice, dodging Peter's heavy backpack. I knew what he was talking about, naturally. And it annoyed me too.

'Stupid idiot,' I muttered, hoping that no one else had noticed. 'Anyway, what do you think? Should I call Delora this afternoon, after school? Just to make sure? I have to anyway, because I've got this money for her.'

137

Peter was red in the face. 'Are you sure she won't want *more* money?' he said.

'I don't know. Maybe not. If she does, we can just wait and see, I guess.'

'I guess.'

And that was that. The bell went, we parted, and I didn't see Peter again until the end of the school day, when we were waiting for the bus. By that time I had already alerted Michelle and Bettina to my plan, and they hadn't objected to it, though Bettina was convinced that she now had Eloise well under control.

'Which means I won't get hungry in the night any more, which means I won't eat too much,' she crowed, as we trooped out of the school gates. 'And if I don't eat too much, I'll lose weight, and if I lose weight, I'll have friends!'

Michelle and I stared at her.

'What do you mean?' I was almost insulted. 'You already have friends.'

'*We're* your friends,' Michelle pointed out, as if Bettina was being incredibly stupid. 'What you weigh doesn't have anything to do with it.'

Bettina went pink.

'Really?' she squeaked.

'Of course.' I nudged her onto the bus, and she bounced on ahead of me, looking pleased even from the back. Just to prove that I wasn't lying, I sat next to her. Michelle dropped into the seat behind me. And Peter . . . well, Peter hesitated. He had been talking to

Serge Blatevsky, who was tugging him into a seat down the front of the bus. He caught my eye, grinned a lopsided grin, and lifted his hand in a half-hearted way before joining Serge.

'What's he doing over there?' Michelle spluttered. 'What about the Exorcists' Club?'

She half rose, but I pulled her back. I knew exactly what Peter was doing, as a matter of fact. And I didn't blame him, though it hurt me a little.

'It's all right,' I said. 'He's a boy. Boys need boys.' What boys *don't* need is other boys teasing them about girls. They hate that. I know they do, because I have a brother. If you want to absolutely enrage Bethan, all you have to do is make jokes about the way he chases Elizabeth Green, sometimes.

'Okay,' I said, taking a deep breath and averting my gaze from the back of Peter's head, 'so what are you going to do, Bettina? Move into your bedroom, again?'

'Of course.'

'Leave a bottle of formula out every night?'

Bettina shrugged. 'Maybe,' she rejoined. 'Or maybe one bottle is all the ghost needed. Maybe it won't be hungry any more.'

'Maybe.' I couldn't really argue with that. It was quite possible.

But somehow I had my doubts.

CHAPTER # *eleven*

I couldn't *believe* it when I walked through our front door. Mum was on the phone, talking to her friend Trish, so even though I was desperate to speak to Delora, I had to hang around, drinking milk and fiddling with the fridge magnets, while Mum arranged a trip to the movies. That very night.

'Well, I can leave it to Ray,' she was saying. 'Yes, Ray can cook them dinner. It's his turn anyway. What? Oh, yes . . . Yes . . . oh, we can grab something there, don't you think? Sure. Hmm? Oh, do you think so?'

The call went on and on. Meanwhile Bethan stampeded into the kitchen, grabbed a muesli bar, and hurled himself out again. I could hear his feet clumping up the stairs. At last Mum put the receiver down. She smiled at me, and asked if I wanted to use the phone.

'Yes, please,' I replied.

'You'll be all right with Ray tonight, won't you?'

'Oh, sure.' I was looking for Delora's number in the family address book, which has many little scraps of paper tucked behind the back cover, and one of my old drawings pasted on the front. I finally reached her on her mobile number.

'You what?' she crackled, when I tried to explain the situation. (It was a very bad connection.)

'We think the ghost in Bettina's room is gone!' I said loudly.

'Did you say ghost?'

'The one in Bettina's room! The hungry force? It was a dead baby!'

'A what? A baby?'

'We think it's gone!'

By the time Delora had grasped what I was trying to tell her, Mum was back in the room, after paying Bethan a little visit. She was leaning against a wall, listening.

'You want me to come over and check? That the energy's gone?' Delora's voice sounded faint through the static. 'Is that what you're asking?'

'Yes, please,' I confirmed. 'Also, I've got your money. Your money for last time.' (Mum had kindly stopped at a bank machine, on our way home from school the previous day.)

'Oh, I won't charge for a follow-up, pet.'

'But you can come? Soon?'

141

'I can come tonight. I'll be passing through. I've got a sitting out that way at six-thirty. I can pick you up at about five-thirty, if you . . . *crackle crackle* . . . else drops you home.'

'Hang on a minute.' I turned to Mum, and in pleading tones gave her an update on the Eloise Amirault case. 'Can I go, Mum? Please? We could eat at five.'

'Ray doesn't get home until five.'

'We could eat then.'

'But – oh all right.' She gave a huge sigh. 'It looks like I'll be cooking after all.'

'Thanks, Mum!'

'But only if you can find someone to drop you home, Allie. Mrs Berich, or Michelle's mum –'

'I know. It's okay. I'll sort it out.'

And I did. After saying goodbye to Delora, I rang the Beriches, and Michelle, and Peter, and they all fell in with my arrangements. Peter's brother promised to drive Peter and Michelle to Bettina's house, while Michelle's mother agreed to pick us all up afterwards. Everything had been settled by five o'clock, at which point dinner was being served and Ray was walking through the front door.

He put his briefcase down, in a dazed fashion, while Mum and I bombarded him with information about our plans.

'I'm going out with Trish tonight, love –'

'And I'm going to Bettina's place. Delora's picking me up –'

'And Trish is picking *me* up, so you'll still have the car –'

'But don't worry, because Michelle's mum will be dropping me home . . .'

Poor Ray. It was a lot to absorb. Mum and I were both talking through mouthfuls of spaghetti, too, and that can't have made us easy to understand. Nevertheless, he nodded as he sat down, and didn't raise any objections. 'Pass the parmesan' was the only thing he said. He's always pretty tired after work.

I really bolted my dinner, that evening. I even beat my brother (and that's saying a lot, believe me). Then I dashed upstairs, cleaned my teeth, and was packing Delora's forty dollars into my purse when she arrived at a quarter to six. I could hear her cockatoo voice from my bedroom, as she joked with Mum.

Because she was late, I scurried to join her as quickly as I could. She was wearing silver boots, this time – like an astronaut. She also wore a silvery sequin skirt and a black halter-neck top, with something printed on it that looked a bit like the Milky Way. Her hair was twisted into a knot, and two enormous silver moons dangled from her ears.

'I know it's a bit way out,' she admitted, when I gaped at her. 'But these clients I'm seeing are a bit way out, too.'

'It's very kind of you to do this,' Mum said, accompanying us out to Delora's beat-up old car. 'I hope the news is good.'

'So do I.' Delora apologised for the junk on the front passenger seat, instructing me to push it all off onto the floor. 'That was a nasty presence in your friend's room,' she added. 'Very strong. One of the worst I've ever encountered.'

'Allie says they got rid of it with a bottle of baby formula,' Mum remarked. She had to stoop to address Delora, who had climbed in behind the steering wheel. 'Is that possible, do you think?'

Delora shrugged. 'I don't know.' She sounded sceptical. 'You never can tell, I suppose – not with the afterlife – but it seems pretty unusual.' She slammed her door shut. 'Got your seatbelt on, darl?'

'Yes.'

'Off we go, then. Bye, Judy!'

'Bye!'

I had never travelled in Delora's car. It was amazing. The whole back seat was piled high with stuff: hats and sandals and magazines and filmy scarves and oil-burners and electricity bills and empty cigarette packets. There were stickers (mostly star-shaped) all over the windows, and a crystal hanging from the rear-view mirror. Poems were written on the ceiling in different-coloured inks.

I would have loved it, except that the whole car stank of cigarette smoke.

'Nice car,' I observed timidly.

'Thank you, pet. It suits me, anyway.'

'What's the crystal for?'

'Protection.'

'Oh.' I remembered the money, then, and dug it out of my purse. Delora told me to stick it in the glove box, but when I opened the glove box, a whole lot of maps and make-up spilled out. So she told me to find her bag, instead.

It wasn't too hard, despite all the clutter.

'So,' I said, having paid my debt and cleared my throat, 'will this be all right for you, Delora?'

'What's that, sweetie?'

'I mean, going into Bettina's bedroom. You said it might be dangerous.'

'Oh, not unless I try to *channel*.' Delora punched at her horn, because the car in front of her had done something stupid. 'I'm not going to *channel*, pet, any more than I did last time. I'll just slip in and see if the energy's still there. Won't take a minute. It was so strong last time I could have taken a *picture*, so I won't need to engage it, or anything.'

'Right.' I didn't quite understand, but was satisfied that Delora hadn't any misgivings about her upcoming visit. Looking around some more, I said: 'Is that a dream-catcher?'

'Pretty, isn't it?'

'Do you *sleep* in here?'

Delora laughed her rasping laugh.

'Not if I can help it,' she replied. 'It doesn't have cruise control, this one – it's a real bomb.'

It was certainly a bumpy sort of car, always jerking

145

to a halt as Delora grappled with the gearstick, cursing under her breath. But we finally made it, and burst into Bettina's house to discover that both Michelle and Peter had already arrived. Astra was there, too, and Mrs Berich, of course. They all looked kind of edgy.

'Hello, everyone!' Delora squawked. I think she was a little nervous herself, after her last visit. 'Just popping in to suss out that bedroom. Allie says it's not Invested any more, is that right?'

Bettina glanced up at her mother, who shifted uncomfortably.

'Maybe not,' Mrs Berich replied, in a sombre voice. Astra's arms were folded across her chest.

'I put a bottle of formula in there,' Bettina volunteered, 'and no one's been hungry since. I mean, not in that bedroom.'

'Is the bottle in there now?' Delora wanted to know, and pursed her lips when Bettina nodded. 'Then take it out for me, will you, pet? There's a good girl.' Once again, while Bettina went to fetch the bottle, Delora turned to Mrs Berich. 'I'll just pop inside for a few minutes, and you won't know I'm here. Mind if I keep the door shut? No? Good. Thank you!'

Seeing her move towards the bedrooms, I asked if she needed anything. But she shook her head.

'Just a few minutes,' she reiterated. 'And a bit of peace.'

She disappeared. I heard a door closing. Bettina, cradling the baby's bottle, returned to the living room, where (I suddenly realised) the entertainment unit no longer supported Michael's little shrine. The baseball cap was gone. So were the trophies, the cheeseboard and the birthday card. Only one of the photographs was left.

'Oh,' I said, before I could stop myself. Everyone noticed what I was looking at, and Astra stepped forward to answer the unspoken question that hung in the air.

'The dead are dead,' she declared, as if she'd been challenged. 'You cannot keep them.'

'You don't want to keep them,' Mrs Berich remarked quietly, watching her sister.

'No. That's right.'

'If you keep them, you have dead babies making trouble in your bedroom.'

'Yes.' Astra looked upset, for a moment, but then blinked and added fiercely: 'Is good Michael is at peace. Peaceful. We don't want him here, like the baby. Poor baby.'

'Poor baby,' Mrs Berich echoed. Obviously her sister had come to accept that the ghost in the bedroom did exist – or had existed, anyway. We were still waiting to find out if it existed any more.

'Would you like drinks?' Mrs Berich suddenly inquired. She waved her hand at the couch. 'Sit down, please.'

'We have lemon cordial,' Bettina began, but was interrupted by Delora's entrance. We were all quite

147

shocked, I think, to see her standing there in the doorway. She blinked a few times, screwing up her eyes against the light.

No one had expected that she would return so soon.

'Well,' she announced, '*something's* certainly happened.'

'That was quick,' said Peter.

'Because it was easy.' Delora approached Mrs Berich, adjusting her top-knot, which was starting to unravel. 'I don't know what you've done, sweetie, but that bedroom is as clean as a whistle.'

'Clean?' Bettina's mum repeated, frowning.

'There's nothing in there.' Delora spoke firmly. 'Not a tweak. Not a glimmer. The energy's *completely* gone.'

'Gone?'

'I don't know if it will stay away,' Delora continued, dragging the strap of her handbag over her shoulder. 'It might do. I can't advise you on that. All I can say is, that room's now safe to sleep in. At this point in time.'

I was amazed. So Bettina had been right after all, and I had been wrong! Then Bettina herself asked a question, before Delora could leave the house.

'So should we keep putting this bottle in there?' she queried. 'Or don't we have to, any more?'

Delora shrugged.

'I don't know. Probably. Unless there's something else you've been doing?' Her gaze flitted from Bettina's face to Astra's and back again. 'Holy water? Anything like that? A purifying ritual of some sort?'

Bettina and her mother shook their heads mutely. I don't think Astra understood what was being said.

'Then it's a mystery,' Delora concluded. 'It could have been the bottle, or it could have been something else, entirely unrelated. I can't help you on that one, I'm afraid.'

'But it *is* gone now?' Mrs Berich interjected, as if she wanted to be absolutely sure. 'The ghost is gone?'

'Oh, quite gone,' said Delora. She smiled, and blew a kiss at me. 'Bye, Allie. Bye, everyone. Gotta go.'

And that was that. It felt funny in the living room, after Delora had left. Everyone was still standing there: Bettina was holding the bottle; Michelle hadn't surrendered the tin of biscuits that she'd brought for Mrs Berich. (Michelle's mother always makes her take a gift of food with her wherever she goes, even if she's coming to my house.) At last Astra said something in Croatian, to her sister, and Mrs Berich grunted.

'So *does* anyone want lemon cordial?' Bettina asked. 'Or tea?'

'No, thank you,' said Peter.

'No, thank you,' I replied.

'Actually, I'd better phone my mum,' Michelle reminded us all. 'So that she can come and get us. Er, by the way, this is for you, Mrs Berich.'

Bettina's mother seemed confused when Michelle placed the tin of biscuits in her hands. But she politely showed Michelle where the phone was, leading her out of the room. After they'd gone, Bettina cleared her throat and said: 'I'll go and put this bottle back.'

'Can we come along?' Peter asked. 'Can we see what it's like, in there?'

'Sure. Okay.' A burst of Croatian from Bettina, aimed at her aunt – who nodded. Next thing Peter and I were following Bettina into her bedroom, which looked exactly the same as it always had. The same blinds were rattling in the window, the same green spread covered the bed, the same junk was strewn over the chest of drawers . . .

It didn't *feel* the same, though. Something was different.

'Have you aired it out?' I inquired. 'Have you been leaving the window open, or something?'

'No,' Bettina responded.

'It seems bigger,' Peter observed. 'Does it seem bigger to you?'

'Not really.' I studied the walls, the carpet, the ceiling. 'You've cleaned the light fitting.'

'No.' Bettina shook her head. 'We haven't touched it.'

Peter, laughed, just as Michelle walked into the room. She asked him what was so funny.

'We are,' he said, with a grin. 'We're all so completely flummoxed. Like – the forces of the universe have converged to change the space/time continuum!'

'Huh?' said Michelle. 'What do you mean?'

'I *mean* that we've solved it without even knowing how!' Peter explained, reverting back to normal English.

Michelle frowned.

'Which is better than not solving it at all,' Michelle snapped, and I added quietly: 'No one claimed to be an expert, Peter. I certainly didn't.'

'Anyway, we do know how,' Bettina objected. 'It was the bottle. Isn't that right?'

'Maybe,' I said. 'Maybe not.'

'But –'

'Delora wasn't sure,' Michelle pointed out. 'We'll never really know.'

'And does it matter?' Peter said. The ghost's gone. That's all that *really* matters.'

I disagreed with him, but I didn't say so. What was the use of reminding him that, unless we could determine exactly what had driven Eloise away, we couldn't be sure that she would *stay* away? If I expressed the fear that she might come back, I would only upset Bettina.

That's why I kept my mouth shut. I just went along with everyone else, admiring Bettina's collection of pencil-sharpeners, selecting one of Michelle's biscuits, and discussing time travel with Peter until Michelle's mum showed up. I said thank you to Mrs Berich very nicely, before climbing into the back seat of Michelle's mum's glossy new four-wheel drive.

It wasn't until I saw the yellow car parked outside our house that I remembered Dad's invitation, and checked my watch with a growing sense of horror.

Seven o'clock.

CHAPTER # twelve

'Oh no,' I murmured.

It all came flooding back to me. The phone call. The dinner plans. My promise to call Dad if there were any problems.

'What's up?' Peter said.

'N-nothing,' I stammered. Michelle's mum was pulling over, rolling to a standstill behind the yellow car. I was tempted to ask if she could please keep going. I didn't want to face Dad. I didn't want to enter the house.

But I had to.

'Bye, Allie.'

'Bye, Allie!'

'Bye.' Slowly I climbed out of my seat and trudged to the front gate. The living-room light was on, but

I couldn't see anyone peering through the downstairs window. The gate creaked as I pushed it. The front door swung open.

It was Ray, thank goodness.

'Hello,' he said.

'Hello.'

'Your father's here.'

I stared up at him, speechless, and he looked gravely down at me. He didn't seem angry, just a bit concerned.

'It's all right, Allie.'

'I forgot!' I squeaked.

'I know. We all forget things sometimes.'

'What we have to do, however,' Dad suddenly cut in, from behind Ray, 'is channel our efforts into remembering the important things, rather than allowing more trivial matters to overwhelm us.'

Dad was waiting in the hall. His hands were plunged deep in his pockets, jingling change and car keys.

'Sorry, Dad,' I muttered.

'It doesn't matter to me, Alethea,' Dad replied. He was obviously upset about something, though. 'It's you I'm worried about. I'm worried that you're going to regret missed opportunities as you grow older.'

'I'm really sorry.'

'So am I. I'm sorry we missed this chance to get acquainted.' He sighed, his fingers still churning around in his pockets. 'Perhaps if I'd been allowed to know you better, I'd understand why you believed that this appointment of yours was so much more important than your time with me.'

All at once, I felt Ray's hand on my shoulder.

'I don't think that's the case, Jim,' Ray said quietly. 'Allie forgot, that's all. Kids forget, sometimes.'

'But my point is that our dinner date was *forgettable*. Far more so than whatever event kept Alethea out tonight.' Dad was frowning. 'I want to find out why that is. Why I'm clearly relegated to the background, here.'

I opened my mouth to explain that he was *very* important. Ray, however, jumped in before me.

'I don't think this is useful, Jim,' he warned. I knew that tone of voice, though I didn't hear it very often.

'Perhaps not for you,' Dad replied dismissively. 'For Alethea I think it's vital. And for me. We have a relationship to explore, and it's crucial that we explore it.' Dad bent down, propping his hands on his knees, so that his face was pretty much level with mine. 'The mind is a very complex entity, Alethea. It's actually quite rare that we "forget" things for no reason. Often what we "forget" can tell us something about our innermost feelings. We repress things we don't want to know or think about.'

I swallowed. Ray's hand tightened on my shoulder.

'Okay, that's enough,' he said. 'This isn't the time or the place. This is something we'll sort out when Judy gets home.'

Dad straightened. The two of them began to address each other way above my head.

'Ray, the last thing I want to do is get confrontational –'

'Good.'

'But this is my daughter –'

'Really?'

'Yes, really.' A pause. 'What are you implying?'

'Well,' Ray said calmly, 'I just think it's odd that you should talk about being *relegated* to the background, when it seems to have been your active *choice* for so many years.'

'I've already indicated that I'm now trying to correct that decision.'

'Well, good. Fine. But let's take it a little more slowly, shall we?'

'Ray, Alethea's already twelve –'

'So she's got plenty of time to sort things out for herself.'

'Not if she continues to deny or suppress any feelings of anger or rejection.'

'Jim,' Ray snapped, 'why don't you put a sock in it?'

By this time I was getting frightened.

'Ray,' I quavered. 'Dad. Don't. I'm sorry.'

'You've nothing to be sorry *for*, love,' Ray retorted, and Dad cocked his head reprovingly.

'Oh, come now,' he said, with a little laugh, 'let's not deny her responsibility for *all* her actions. She did stand me up, Ray – not that I regard that as a terrible sin –'

'Allie, go upstairs, please.'

'Ray, she's not a child –'

155

'*Of course she's a bloody child!*'

'Ray, please.' Dad lifted his hands. 'What I mean is, she's entering puberty, she's growing up –'

'Allie, will you go upstairs? You really don't want to hear this.'

'You know Ray, if we're going to throw our weight about, may I just point out that *I* am Alethea's father –'

'Since when?'

'Oh, don't!' I cried. 'Please!' I was terrified. Ray seemed to sense that, because his grip suddenly relaxed, and he placed his other hand on my hair.

'Sorry, love,' he said, in a slightly shaky voice. 'Sorry. Shouldn't carry on like this, eh?'

'Yes, there's nothing to be gained by raised voices or personal accusations,' Dad agreed. 'What we have to do is discuss this calmly, rationally, with goodwill, so that we can get to the bottom of our difficulties –'

'Not tonight,' Ray interrupted. 'Allie, you haven't had your shower. Why don't you go up and have it now? Before Mum gets back?'

I hesitated.

'Ray, if she doesn't want to –'

'I do! I do! Just . . .' I didn't know how to say it. 'Just don't – don't get mad, okay?'

'We won't get mad,' Ray assured me. 'It's all right.'

'Alethea, I've always held the view that anger is the toxic waste of our natural emotional balance, and should be regarded as purposeless.'

So I went upstairs. I went slowly, dragging my feet,

listening hard for any raised voices down below. But there were no shouts or banging doors, there was only a low rumble of conversation. By the time I reached my bedroom, I couldn't even hear that.

Bethan was in his own little cave, which he's managed to trash since we moved in. After we got rid of Eglantine, it was clean and airy; now the white walls are plastered with football and skateboarding posters, the polished floor is invisible beneath piles of toys and clothes, and dirty old sneakers are oozing out from under the bed in an unstoppable tide.

'What's going on?' Bethan inquired, when he saw me. 'Were you supposed to go out with Dad, or something?'

I nodded.

'That's what he said.' Bethan nodded, satisfied. 'Did you forget?'

'Yes.'

Bethan wrinkled up his nose. He was lying on the bed, taking apart one of his plastic monster constructions, which was half dinosaur, half bulldozer.

'He wants *me* to go out, next time,' Bethan complained. 'I don't want to go to one of those yukky places with the fried slugs.'

'What fried slugs?'

'You know. That okra stuff.'

'Oh.'

'Why won't he take us to Australia's Wonderland, or something? I don't want to go with him and eat burny food in that smelly house.'

Bethan sees things so simply. It's all so straight-forward, for him.

'But don't you think we ought to?' I asked – really wanting to know. I was standing in the doorway, my ears still cocked for sounds of an argument downstairs. 'I mean, he's our dad. We should *want* to go with him.'

'I do want to go with him. When he goes somewhere that's *fun*.' Bethan tightened a screw. 'Stupid thing,' he said, but he was talking to the toy monster.

I left him there, retreating into my bedroom. Already the tears were pricking at my eyes; I wanted to be safe behind my locked bedroom door before I let the first sobs escape. It was *awful*. I felt so *guilty*. Not because I had forgotten the dinner – though I was ashamed of myself for being so disorganised – but because Dad was right. There *was* a reason why his invitation had slipped my mind; why it had taken a backseat to my arrangements with Delora. It was because I really didn't want to be with Dad. I hated going out with him. I hated having him around. I wanted him to leave and never come back. That was the reason why I didn't want to live with him. Ever.

I hadn't wanted to admit it, even to myself, but I couldn't pretend any more.

I was bawling my eyes out when the phone rang. I could hear it because there's an extension upstairs, in the main bedroom. But I was crying too hard to answer it – and Bethan never answers phones.

There were four rings, then silence. After a while, footsteps sounded on the stairs.

'Allie?' Ray called. 'Phone for you!'

I couldn't reply. My voice would have wobbled.

'Allie?' More footsteps, approaching my bedroom. The door handle turned, but the door was locked. 'Allie, are you all right?'

I got up, and went to unlock the door. I had to. When Ray saw my face, his own face twisted up.

'Oh, baby,' he said. 'It's all right. He's gone now.'

'He's angry with me!' I wailed.

'No, he's not. Come here.' Ray hugged me tight. 'Allie, it's not the end of the world. I told you – everyone forgets things. Jim used to forget your birthday, sometimes, don't you remember?' A pause. 'It didn't mean he doesn't love you.'

'It does!' I croaked. 'It does!'

'No –'

'Yes. Because – because –'

'Hang on.' Ray pulled me inside my room, shutting the door behind him. He took me to sit on the bed. 'Now, what's wrong? Eh? Tell me.'

'I – I –'

'Take it slowly.'

'I don't even *like* him!' The truth was out. 'I don't even like my own dad!'

There was a long silence. At last Ray said, 'Well, I'm not surprised. He's not very likeable.'

'You shouldn't say that!' I sobbed.

'No. You're right. I shouldn't.' Ray put his arm around me again, squeezing my shoulders. 'Allie,' he sighed, into my hair, 'your father's paid you almost no attention since you were four years old. Now, suddenly he turns up, expecting you to want to be with him, and to do what he says. It's unreasonable, Allie. *He's* being unreasonable, not you. You're doing the best you can.'

'But I – but so is he. Now. I feel so bad. I get so *cross.*'

'There's nothing wrong with that.'

I wiped my eyes, pulling away from him. 'Really?'

'Really.'

'But what am I going to say?' I sniffed. 'When he asks why I forgot? When he asks what it is that I'm not admitting?'

'Oh, he won't,' Ray interrupted, speaking very firmly and dryly. His calm, dark gaze flickered for an instant. 'Believe me, your father won't say another word on the subject.'

'How do you know?'

'Because your mum and I will make sure he doesn't.'

'How?'

'Never you mind.'

Troubled, I studied his expression, which was hard to read. Then he smiled, and tucked some hair behind my left ear.

'Don't look so worried, Allie. It'll be all right. You should be civil – of course you should – but don't worry about how your father feels, or what he wants. That's his business, not yours. You don't owe him anything – not until he earns a place in this family. Your job is to give him the chance. That's all.'

I absorbed this, turning it over in my head. At last I admitted: 'I don't feel like he's my father, Ray. *You're* more like my father than he is.'

'Well . . . that's how I feel, too,' Ray replied, very softly.

'So what am I supposed to do?'

'Nothing.' He kissed my forehead. 'It's your dad's job to work out what he wants to be. He can't come back here expecting to revive something that's been dead for years, Allie. He has to create something new.'

'And – and I won't have to live with him?' I faltered.

'Live with him?' Ray stared. 'Who said anything about living with him?'

'It happens, doesn't it? Kids have to go from one house to the other, all the time? When their parents get divorced?'

Ray's mouth twisted. 'You're talking about custody,' he said. 'Shared custody.'

'I guess . . .'

Ray took a deep breath. He rubbed his nose, and scratched his head. 'Allie,' he sighed at last, 'I won't try to kid you. Your father *might* ask for shared custody. If he does, we'll have to talk about it. He won't take it to court, that's for sure.' Ray's voice was flat. 'If he does, he'll have to explain the last eight years. I don't think he'll be able to.'

'But I don't *want* to live with him, Ray!'

'Of course you don't. Why should you? Maybe one day you will, if he makes an effort.' Ray squeezed me again. 'Just tell him how you feel, Allie. If he asks you to move in, just tell him how you feel, and he'll have to deal with it. That's all you can do. That's all you should *have* to do. Remember – your mum and I don't want you to be unhappy, and neither does your dad. We'll all make sure that you're happy.'

I thought about what Ray had said, as he rocked me back and forth. I'd been worrying about Dad for such a long time; it felt wonderful to have aired all my worries, at last. Once I'd admitted the truth to myself, I'd finally been able to talk. What a relief!

'Now,' said Ray, and his arm dropped from my shoulders. 'Are you up to a conversation with Peter, or shall I say that you'll call him back?'

'Oh!' Once again, my memory had let me down. I'd forgotten all about the phone call. 'Oh, no, I'll talk to him!'

'Are you sure?'

'Yes, yes!' I grabbed a tissue from my bedside cabinet, and rubbed it over my face. Ray got up.

'You can take the call in our bedroom, if you like,' he offered. 'More privacy.'

He didn't say this in the annoying way that Tony Karavias might have said it, so I didn't know if he was trying to hint at something or not. Nevertheless, I was anxious that he not get the wrong idea. After all, Peter wasn't my *boyfriend*.

'I don't need privacy, Ray.'

'Oh, I think you do,' Ray responded, in quite a serious tone. 'Everyone needs a bit of privacy. At least, that's what I told your father.' He opened the door for me. 'There you go.'

Poor Peter had been waiting for such a long time that the first thing he said, after I greeted him, was: 'Where were you, in the toilet?'

'No, I – no.'

'What's wrong?' He must have heard me sniffling and snuffling. 'Are you all right?'

'I'm okay. My dad – there's some stuff with my dad. He was going to take me out to dinner.'

'Your *dad*?' Peter exclaimed. 'But I thought your dad was in Thailand!'

Before I knew it, I had told him everything – it all spilled out in a great gush of words. Peter listened. He grunted sympathetically now and then, but didn't comment until I had finished. Then he said: 'Well, Ray is right.'

'Do you think so?'

'Course he is! It's like Astra, isn't it? She was trying to revive something that had been dead for years –'

'Some*one*, you mean.'

'Whatever. The point is, you can't. You just can't.'

'But –'

'And don't say "what about Eloise?", because she's a perfect example of how bad it can get, when dead

163

things are still cluttering up your life.' Peter took a deep breath, which I could hear even over the phone. 'Speaking of which,' he added, 'my mum just came home from her evening shift, and guess what?'

'What?'

'It's unbelievable.'

'*What*, Peter?'

'Well, she decided to ask her manager about Terri Amirault, today,' Peter began, 'just to see if she was allowed to give out any information, and when she raised the subject, her manager went white – like, totally freaked – and couldn't *believe* the coincidence –'

'*What* coincidence? Peter!'

'I'm telling you. Calm down.' He was enjoying the build-up, though; I could sense it. He wanted to drag it out. 'Apparently, yesterday afternoon, the manager got a phone call from this person he knows – a police officer, or something, I'm not sure – to say that Terri Amirault, who'd been living in a halfway house, I think, a kind of group home in Malabar somewhere –'

'Where, Peter? Did you get the address?'

'No, I didn't, and it doesn't matter, because guess what?' A dramatic pause. 'She's dead.'

'What?'

'She died yesterday. Of a drug overdose.'

I gasped. 'Oh, my God.'

'*Yesterday*, Allie. Think about it.'

I *was* thinking about it. I was thinking about how horrible life could be, with people dying all over the place. Babies. Cousins. Poor drug addicts who were obviously very, very unhappy.

It made me realise how small my own problems were, in comparison.

'Think about it, Allie,' Peter said again. 'This happened the very day that Eloise disappeared. It makes sense, doesn't it? She got what she wanted. She got her mother.'

'Maybe.'

'Oh, come on!' Peter was becoming excited. 'It *has* to be that! Terri's joined her in . . . well, wherever she is. The afterlife. Don't you think?'

'I suppose so.'

'I *know* so,' Peter declared firmly. 'You were right. It wasn't the formula. You've got a real instinct for these things, haven't you? Allie? What's wrong?'

'Oh, I don't know.' I was a bit wrung out, and tired of messing around with ghosts. For the first time, I could see myself through other people's eyes. It really *was* weird to be chasing ghosts for a hobby – weird and not very healthy, either. It meant you were always dealing with death and dead people. Horrible things.

'Look, I'm having second thoughts about the Exorcists' Club,' I confessed. 'I don't know if it's a good idea. This one was a bit close to the bone, for me, and anyway, what good does it do? Really?'

'Are you kidding?' Peter's tone was almost horrified. 'It's a terrific idea!'

'But it's so depressing, Peter –'

165

'No, it's not! It's – it's . . .' He seemed to be search-ing for an impressive and convincing term. 'It's *liberating*,' he finally said. 'Look how good Bettina's feeling now! We've solved her problem for her!'

I started to shake my head, even though he couldn't see me. 'No we didn't. It solved itself,' I pointed out.

'But she knows why she was fat, now. She knows it wasn't her fault. And she's excited about getting back to normal, and having friends . . .' Peter faltered, suddenly; I wondered if he had remembered what he'd said to me, once, in the bus line. 'She's not dumb, you know,' he admitted. 'You were right about that, as well. I reckon you're right about everything. You're so smart, Allie.'

And embarrassed, too. My face grew hot. 'Yeah, right,' I mumbled.

'It's true. You can't resign from the Exorcists' Club. How would we be able to help people without you? It's *important* that you stay. It's – like – community service.'

I don't know anyone who wouldn't have been flat-tered by praise like this. It made me relax, for some reason; I felt much better, as if I'd been promised a week at Disney World.

'You reckon?' I said.

'Absolutely.'

'And *you* still believe in the Exorcists' Club?'

'Totally,' said Peter.

I thought for a moment. 'And does that mean you'll

sit with us on the bus, from now on?' I queried, unable to stop myself, though I knew that I was being a bit unfair. I was teasing him, actually, in a funny sort of way.

When he didn't immediately reply, I got anxious, and gabbled: 'It's okay, I don't mind or anything, I just didn't know if we should hold proper meetings –'

'Actually,' Peter broke in, with a hint of defiance, 'I do think we should hold meetings on the bus. Why not? We're all there. We've got plenty to talk about. Why bother holding meetings at each other's houses when we don't have to?'

'Right. Okay.' I was *very* pleased. 'Good!'

'Uh, which isn't to say we can't go to each other's houses,' Peter quickly amended. I could hear him breathing heavily, as if he was struggling with shoe-laces. 'In fact my mum was asking if you wanted to come around, some time. I said I'd ask you.'

'Sure. Great,' I replied awkwardly. 'If *you* don't mind.'

'I don't mind.'

'Okay. Um . . . when?'

'Tomorrow?'

'Okay. I'll ask Mum.'

'Okay.'

I felt exhausted, like someone who had just run an enormous race. But it was happy exhausted. Sense-of-achievement exhausted. When I said goodbye, and hung up, I realised that the world was looking a lot brighter than it had half an hour before.

He's a very good friend, is Peter. So is Michelle, of course. When I told *her* about my dad the next day, she advised me not to worry about him. If I played my cards right, she said, I'd have him eating out of my hand.

'If you don't like him, let him know it. Then he'll be running around buying you things. Taking you out places. It'll be great.'

'He's already taken us out,' I replied doubtfully. 'To that Egyptian restaurant.'

'No, no, I'm talking about *good* places. Allie, I know what I'm talking about. Believe me.' Michelle laid a hand on my arm. She gazed into my eyes. 'This could be very good for you. He's been away all this time – he owes you everything you can get out of him. Just remember: the ruder you are, the guiltier he'll feel.'

I thanked her, because she was trying to help me, but I didn't take her advice. It seemed to me that she was talking about her own family, rather than mine. And anyway, as Bettina pointed out, I was really quite lucky that my dad was interested enough to return to Australia. Bettina's father wasn't. He was more interested in his new family, on the other side of the world.

'At least your dad cares,' she said wistfully. 'At least you can see him, now. I haven't seen my dad for five years.'

Poor Bettina. I can't help feeling sorry for her, even though she does laugh and talk more, these days. Ever since she joined the Exorcists' Club, she's been a lot happier. Oh, yes, the Exorcists' Club is still going. There are still only four members, and we still haven't exorcised anything, yet. Not officially. We certainly didn't have anything to do with the disappearance of Eloise, which was just a stroke of luck. In fact, I wasn't thoroughly convinced that she had disappeared for good, until something happened at Bettina's house the other day.

The rest of us were on the bus when we heard. It was the usual morning update. Bettina wanted to talk about it as soon as we appeared, but Michelle and I made her wait for Peter. We always do that, now. We've drawn up rules about it.

'So,' I said, after Peter had finally joined us. 'What's the big news?'

'Oh, it's not big,' Bettina admitted. She was knitting her brows. 'At least, I don't know. It's funny . . .'

'What's funny?' Michelle said impatiently. 'Don't tell me Eloise is back?'

'Oh, *no*. No. It's just that . . . well, yesterday Mum was looking for this rag that used to be in the laundry. But it's disappeared. And we don't know how.'

Peter and Michelle and I rolled our eyes at each other.

'So you've got a missing *rag*,' Peter drawled. 'I see.' If you think he was being too sarcastic, I should tell you that Bettina has gotten very jumpy about ghosts and things. She seems to think that the school library is haunted, nowadays.

169

'Yes, but it wasn't just any rag,' Bettina insisted. 'We were talking to Astra about it, and she said it was a baby's blanket. A dirty old baby's blanket, with pink rabbits on it. And no one's seen it since Eloise vanished. Even though we always lock the laundry, because of the boys next door. They used to get in and pee on the washing machine.'

'Yuk!' Michelle exclaimed. 'How revolting.'

'So what do you think, Allie?' Bettina fixed her earnest brown gaze on my face. 'Do you think – do you think Eloise might have taken that blanket with her, when she left?'

I thought about it. I thought about Eloise and Eglantine. I thought about all the people living in Bettina's house. Finally, I thought about Delora, and her views on my instincts.

'It's possible,' I said. 'Anything's possible.'

If there's one thing I've learned, after dealing with so many ghosts, it's that anything – but *anything* – is possible.

CATHERINE JINKS was born in Brisbane in 1963 and grew up in Sydney and Papua New Guinea. She studied medieval history at university, and her love of reading led her to become a writer. She lives in the Blue Mountains in New South Wales with her Canadian husband, Peter, and her daughter, Hannah.

Catherine Jinks is the author of over twenty books for children and adults, including the award-winning Pagan series.

Pagan's
Daughter

CATHERINE
JINKS

A mysterious past, a desperate fight, an unforgettable adventure